The Secret of Bailey's

Chase

Quake

THE SECRET OF BAILEY'S CHASE
A Quake Book
Shakin' Up Young Readers!

First Quake paperback printing / 2008

Special thanks to
© Carolyn McGehee
for the drawings used inside this book.

QUAKE

is a division of
Echelon Press, LLC
9735 Country Meadows Lane 1-D
Laurel, MD 20723
www.quakeme.com

13-Digit ISBN: 978-1-59080-577-0
10-Digit ISBN: 1-59080-577-1
eBook: 1-59080-578-X

PRINTED IN THE UNITED STATES OF AMERICA
10 9 8 7 6 5 4 3 2 1

ALSO BY MARLIS DAY

Why Johnny Died

Death of a Hoosier Schoolmaster

The Curriculum Murders

This book is dedicated to Abbie and all the other Girl Scouts who loved Camp Wildwood.

ACKNOWLEDGEMENTS

I want to thank Karen Syed and the team at Echelon Press for believing in me and making this all possible. I also wish to thank Kat Thompson, senior editor, whose diligent search for dangling participles and wandering body parts kept me busy making corrections. Her valuable assistance made this book the best it could be. I am forever in debt to friends and family who read early manuscripts–their support keeps me going. I am grateful to Richard Day, local historian, for sharing information regarding early justice in the community, to which I applied my own dramatic touch. I earnestly thank the kind people of Vincennes, Indiana, for allowing me to borrow their historic sites and favorite son, and temporarily move them to the fictitious town of Bailey's Chase for this novel. As always, I remember and thank my late parents for instilling in me a great love of books. Most of all, I am grateful to my beloved husband, book handler, and traveling partner, D.J. He's always there, making my life easier.

Prologue

A very long time ago, right in the middle of our country there lived an old woman named Granny Bailey. I'm quite sure she had another, more proper name, but everyone in her river town called her Granny Bailey. Some people said she had unusual abilities, some people said she had mysterious gifts, and some people said nothing at all, thinking her quite normal.

But nobody ever said she was a witch, because she was so very kind and gentle.

People didn't know where Granny had come from, but everyone seemed to know she had been born with snow-white hair and piercing azure eyes that changed shades of blue like a kaleidoscope. They knew she had nearly always walked with a limp. As a young girl she was struck by lightning one day as she played in the woods. After that, the stories said she slightly glowed in the dark and her white hair seemed to radiate from her head like sunrays, but some claimed it was just static electricity.

Everyone knew she lived in a cabin at the edge of the big woods. And everyone remembered, or knew someone who remembered, running up the long, grassy path to

Granny's door when they were children. There used to be a sign, the people recalled. A sign showing the way. 'Bailey's Chase', it said, because in the old days 'chase' meant a country path to somebody's house. It was a friendly cabin, lopsided with windows in strange places, some too high to see into, with others knee-level, which made you stoop over to peek in. The townspeople liked to go there because they could always count on a cup of herbal tea and a muffin, as well as an interesting story when they visited Granny.

Some said that Granny could always tell when something bad was going to happen, like a skunk falling down someone's well or a bear eating an innocent blackberry picker as she filled her basket. Others called it coincidence.

Most folks agreed Granny had a way of seeing right through people, and always knew when someone was being dishonest or deceitful. Everyone agreed she could draw fire from a burn, wish warts away, and always choose exactly the right spot to dig a well.

It was a common fact she kept wild birds for pets and spent a lot of time in the woods talking to the animals and collecting roots and leaves for her homemade medicines. According to the stories, many parents visited her cabin in the middle of the night to get medicine for a sick child. She always seemed to know they were coming and was ready with just the right medicine.

A few people still left around believed the old tales

about fires that started just because Granny stared long and hard at someone's woodpile, or that she could tell what the animals said as she walked past them on her daily strolls through the little town on the river.

Granny Bailey was so special in the hearts of the people that when they decided to rename their town due to it outgrowing its boundaries and lapping over onto other small towns, they named it Bailey's Chase in her honor. They didn't think their town would ever see anybody with Granny's special gift again. They thought the gift died when she did and was buried with her.

People didn't realize Granny's special gift didn't get passed on to anybody in particular because that lightning strike split her genes and chromosomes in half and jumbled them every which way. So her special gift didn't pass on to one certain relative, to be noticed and discussed by everyone. Instead, it broke into two neat parcels, bounced around hither and yon, skipped several generations, and finally landed inside two great-great-great-grandchildren.

Those lucky two recipients, unfortunately, could do nothing with half of a gift. In fact, they didn't even have a clue that they *had* a gift. A half gift is actually like having no gift.

One-half of the special gift belonged to Alexandria Greyling Bailey. Her parents lived in a big city and had some difficulty deciding what to name their only child. After fretting and fussing over it for a while, they gave her the first name of one grandmother and the second name of the other grandmother and that was that. Since she turned out to be a dark and brooding child, they called her Grey. Although she didn't say a lot, fantastic thoughts raced through her head most of the time. Talking took her away from the wild and wonderful scenes that played in the daydream theater of her mind.

The other half of the special gift ended up inside of Grey's distant cousin, a lively girl named Amaryllis Bailey. Since she had been able to sit up, her family had nicknamed her Sparky, because she was so energetic and bouncy.

Sparky had loved to talk and make people laugh ever since she noticed people's responses when she made raspberry noises as a baby. By the time she started the second grade, everybody thought Sparky would surely grow up to become either president or one of those people who climb mountains, just to prove they can, because nothing else she could do would use up all that energy.

Even though Grey and Sparky were cousins they really didn't know each other. This is not a surprising fact, since Sparky lived in the middle of the country and Grey lived way off near the ocean. Their parents brought them together at a family reunion as infants, but of course, neither of them could remember it. Later, when they were around three, someone photographed them together at a family wedding, but they only had vague memories of that event.

Then, in a terrible accident, a flash flood swept Grey's parents away. Suddenly an orphan, Grey was forced to choose between a boarding school run by people named 'Mrs. Hardwick' and 'Dr. Zoofram,' or a trial stay with distant relatives. Grey chose to try a stay with the relatives, knowing where the other story was likely to lead, because she had read so many books about orphans who went to boarding schools and regretted it. So the girl cousins, these almost-strangers now going on eleven, would soon live together like sisters. Soon the two halves of Granny Bailey's unusual gift would finally come together.

Chapter One

The child lay crumpled on her bags. She had tried to stay awake, but the long trip had worn her out. First the taxi ride to the airport, then the flight across the country, then the bus ride, and finally a long, slow trip in the little boat. She always tried to look her best and cope with situations, no matter how boring or wretched. But you mustn't feel sorry for the girl, even though she was an orphan, because she was the type of person who faced every event in her life as a new adventure.

On the plane ride, after she had finished reading *Anne of Green Gables* for the umpteenth time, she promised herself that when she grew up and wrote children's books, she would definitely make the characters more daring. For the remainder of the flight, she had entertained herself by creating names for the other passengers around her. She decided that the incredibly boring man next to her should be called Mr. Wilheim Q. Stufflebeem. The quiet, thin woman across the aisle should be Alfreida Mae Pinchnose. And the red-haired freckled five-year-old boy who kept noisily running up the aisle should simply be Bratface.

"Alexandria Greyling Bailey," called a voice in the

warm darkness.

Grey opened her eyes and answered groggily, "Yes?" She tried to sound grown-up and in charge of the situation. She couldn't see a thing, because her hair had drooped over her eyes. The boat's motor had stopped. She thought they must be arriving…finally.

"Riverside Station, Bailey's Chase," the man announced as if the boat was full of people instead of just one exhausted little girl.

"Thank you," Grey said as she pushed the hair away from her eyes. She scrambled to her feet and brushed off her clothes, since she had always been taught to be neat and mannerly. Looking down, she noticed the wrinkles in her pants, but she could do nothing about that, so she tried not to think about it. Then she noticed the spot on her blouse. Probably tomato sauce from the spaghetti they served on the plane, she thought. Although she dabbed at it with a tissue it wouldn't budge. Great, she thought, I'm going to meet my relatives looking like a mess.

Suddenly, Grey remembered seeing people tip others who helped them and briefly wondered if she should tip this man who delivered her to the town of Bailey's Chase. Being the only passenger, she couldn't watch and see what other people did. She'd never been on a little boat like this before, on the little river in the dark, so she had no experience to fall back on. She was confused and felt as if she'd wandered into a movie about a brave pioneer girl searching up and down the Mississippi River for her baby brother, who had been stolen by Indians or something. Except she didn't have a baby brother or any brothers, or sisters, for that matter. Plus, this wasn't the Mississippi River and she didn't feel very brave. She felt sleepy.

Across the dark, quiet water she saw a wooden building with a long platform at the river's edge. On the platform hung a sign with ornate, swirling gold letters on black that read 'Riverside'. The building behind the sign was full of shadows and seemed asleep in the summer moonlight. The platform was brightly lit and didn't seem asleep at all. At the end where the boat would soon land, she saw a group of people. They all waved at the boat. She noticed their blond hair and full friendly faces. The bright platform lights made their hair shine yellow and silver as they moved around.

These must be the other Baileys, she decided. Her blood relatives. Total strangers, but family, even if she didn't look anything like them. Grey raked her fingers through her own long, chestnut-colored curls. She wanted to look her best, even with the spaghetti sauce on her blouse and the weird dents in her face from sleeping on her luggage.

"Better sit down, miss," the captain said. "There will be a bump when we hit the landing." Adults always said things like that to kids, she thought, when they would never say it to adults, who were much more likely to lose their balance and fall.

Grey didn't sit but held onto a bench in the boat's

little cabin with one hand, as she fumbled with her backpack with the other. Folded beside her purse and favorite book lay a copy of the instructions from Susan Briner, her parents' lawyer. Her lawyer, now. Grey really didn't need to read the instructions again; she knew them by heart. The last line merely read: Meet Baileys at Riverside Station, Bailey's Chase, 11:45 P.M. Well, she thought, this is it, the end of a very long journey and the start of a new adventure.

Straightening her shoulders and feeling a little nervous, Grey reminded herself that she didn't have to stay. She had options. She could call Susan, the lawyer, at any time, and Susan would arrange for her to come back to the city. She could go to a boarding school, Susan had said, and spend summers at a camp or something. It was up to her, but Susan had thought Grey should get to know these Baileys, her only family, before making any decisions. Her parents would want her to do this. Grey thought it strange how adults always thought they knew what was best, even though she saw how many of them had totally messed-up lives.

"There's a girl, a cousin named Amaryllis, who's just your age," Susan had mentioned, while shuffling papers on the desk in her office back in the city. "That might be fun."

"Amaryllis," Grey had said, making a face. "What kind of a name is Amaryllis?"

"Well, actually," the lawyer had said, "it's the name

of a flower. It grows from a bulb, I think. I can't imagine naming a child that, but remember, Bailey's Chase is a long way from here. Maybe everybody there names their children for flowering bulbs." She had glanced at Grey and said, "You know, Tulip, Daffodil, Hyacinth?"

Grey had laughed. Susan could always make her laugh. "So," she had pondered, "what would they name the boys?"

"Wow, good question," Susan had replied. "Maybe...Billy of the Valley?"

Grey smiled at the memory as the boat hit the landing with a lurch. A big, blond man grabbed the ropes and tied the boat to metal clamps along the edge of the landing. Then Grey remembered her manners and the tipping question, and grabbed her purse.

"Um, I, uh, enjoyed the trip," she told the captain as she fumbled with her purse. "Thank you so much for...."

"My pleasure," he said with a smile, pushing her toward the platform. "My grandmother told me stories about Granny Bailey when I was a child. No tipping allowed on this trip. My pleasure to bring you." With that he carefully handed her over the side of the little boat and into the bright lights. She didn't understand the grandmother business, but she was too busy to think about it. She was about to meet her relatives–these people who had invited her to come and live with them.

The big blond man stepped forward and said in a

kind voice, "I'm your Uncle Fred." Grey nodded and put her hand out in case he wanted to shake hands with her. Before he could notice it, the woman stepped around him and smiled as she said, "And I'm your Aunt Liz." She hugged Grey warmly. Grey allowed herself to be hugged. She was glad no one kissed her; she didn't much like being kissed.

Grey knew they weren't actually her uncle and aunt, but she was glad to know what to call them. She had been taught to never call adults by their first names. Uncle Fred and Aunt Liz, she thought. That would work.

"Yes," Grey answered in her best voice, trying to look cheerful and interesting even though she was so tired she felt as floppy and clumsy as a puppet. "I'm so pleased to meet you."

After that, she met several Bailey cousins who seemed much older than she. She instantly forgot their names. Two boys and two girls, teenagers or maybe in college already, she decided. None of them looked too interesting, but none were named for plants and she was glad about that.

"And over here is your cousin, Am..." Her uncle suddenly stopped and called in a firm tone, "Amaryllis, front and center!" Then Grey noticed a smaller girl hanging over the side of the landing, poking at the water with a stick. The girl turned and came across the landing to meet her cousin, wiping her wet hands on her T-shirt.

The aunt said something in the way of introductions,

but Grey didn't hear a word she said. She stood with her mouth open, staring at the grinning, brown-eyed girl her own age, ten or so. It looked as if her hair was on fire! The blonde curls flashed and sparked in the night breeze, but Grey didn't see any smoke. Dumfounded, she continued to stare in disbelief.

"Hi, I'm Sparky," the girl said, holding out her hand and staring curiously at Grey's face.

"Do you know that your hair's on *fire*?" Grey asked while shaking hands. Nobody else seemed to notice anything out of the ordinary. She thought she must be tired and seeing things. Hallucinating, that's what people called it. Grey had read about people hallucinating when they got too tired, but she had never done it. She shook her head and blinked, making sure she was awake.

"My hair's not on fire," the girl said with a giggle, running a hand through her hair just to prove it. Grey continued to stare, amazed at the sight.

The girl suddenly leaned forward, stared directly into Grey's eyes, and said, "Your eyes are funny though. They just changed colors!"

Grey thought this cousin was terribly rude to call her eyes *funny*. All of her life people had told her what beautiful blue eyes she had. She glanced toward the rest of the family to see if anyone intended to scold this bouncy girl in front of her, but everyone continued talking and moving around, seeing about those necessary things that adults always have to do.

Taking a deep breath, Grey said, "My eyes are *not* funny. They are blue and they don't change. But you *do* have sparks in your hair, and I'm not kidding. Real sparks. Look!"

Behind them was a window in the shingled wall of the station, and Grey turned the girl around so she could see her reflection in the glass. Grey could see herself, too. The glass reflected two blurry girls, about the same size. One had yellow and orange sparks flashing in her hair, and the other had eyes that started out gray-blue and then turned navy blue and then aqua.

Grey couldn't help staring at their reflections and watching her own eyes. Astounded, she again wondered if she was hallucinating or in the middle of a dream. Sparky said nothing but stared at the reflections with her mouth open.

Just then, a man in a black suit with a black vest and black tie came out of the station and called, "All abooaarrd!" He wore a black hat like a round box with a short, shiny brim. It looked like a train conductor's hat.

Grey thought he meant the ferryboat was leaving, not that anyone waited to get on it. The captain and Uncle Fred and the two oldest cousins were still talking and unloading her bags. They seemed in no hurry. The boat wasn't leaving. Then the man in the black suit looked at a watch on a gold chain he pulled from his vest, and nodded.

"Midnight Express, right on time," he called in a

boisterous voice. He appeared very pleased about the 'right on time' part. "All abooaarrd!"

Confused, Grey looked closely at the station. It looked like a train station, except there wasn't any train and what stopped there were boats. A train station on a moonlit river with a stationmaster announcing trains that weren't there at all. Grey shivered a little, despite the August heat. She still had on the jacket she'd worn on the plane because planes were always cold, and then she'd left it on because of the mosquitoes on the river. Even in the jacket she felt suddenly chilled. Everything about this place seemed so strange to her.

Grey had almost forgotten about the cousin standing by her until she said somewhat cautiously, "Your eyes are so dark now they don't have any color at all." Listening hard, Grey tried to concentrate on her cousin's words, but they made no sense. This whole place wasn't making any sense and that wasn't okay. Things that made no sense always made her feel dizzy. Sometimes they made her angry, too. Or scared.

"Uncle Fred," she asked, trying to sound polite. "Why is he calling 'All aboard' for a train when there's no train here? There aren't even any tracks. There's only water."

"Oh, this is just the station, Riverside Station," her uncle answered as if nothing were out of the ordinary. "It's always been here."

Grey felt a lump in her throat and tears filled her eyes. Her uncle's answer didn't answer anything, didn't say anything. It didn't make any sense and that made her feel dizzy and sick. This place is crazy, she decided. She wiped her eyes with the back of her hand and swallowed hard to try to get rid of the big lump in her throat. She wanted to go home.

"It's the station for the *carousel*," the other girl whispered, sliding a suntanned arm across Grey's shoulders and pointing through the station doors. "See?"

Past the stationmaster's desk a wide, arched doorway led into a big round room with open sides. In the middle of the room Grey could see a darkened carousel. The animals posed silent, shadowy shapes, but in a stripe of moonlight she thought she recognized a giraffe and a pig decorated with carved flowers and ribbons. She glanced at the cousin standing beside her. Her blonde hair continued to throw sparks.

Unable to not mention it, Grey remarked with interest, "Your hair is still…doing that. You *are* kind of sparky."

"Wow, bloody," said the girl.

"Why did you say 'bloody'?"

"Oh, well, it's English, like swearing in English, you know? I mean from England English. Mom freaks out every time I use some of the words the older kids say, so I decided to swear in English, see? Our ancestors are from there, so Mom said she'd let it go as long as I didn't say it at school."

While Grey thought carefully about the swearing

issue, Sparky suddenly changed the subject and said, "Hey, do you want to ride?"

"Ride what?"

"The bloody *carousel,*" Sparky answered, and grabbed Grey's hand. "That's what he meant by 'The Midnight Express'. It's midnight and we get to ride. Only kids ten and under can ride. Once you turn eleven it's over; you can't ride anymore. But we're not eleven yet, so we can, and tonight we have it all to ourselves. There's even a bubble machine, but it only gets turned on for special occasions. Come on!"

As Grey allowed herself to be pulled inside, a thousand lights began to twinkle all over the carousel. At the top hung oval mirrors and the carved, painted faces of jesters. They looked like jokers in a big deck of cards. She thought for a second that one of them winked at her, but that couldn't be, even in this crazy place.

"First a march and then a waltz, I think," said the stationmaster, opening a little gate in the fence surrounding the carousel. Grey heard a groaning sound from behind the painted panels in the middle of the circular ride. It sounded like the yawning of a sleepy giant. Then it turned into breathy, wonderful music.

"'American Patrol,'" the stationmaster announced proudly. "A fine march for an American carousel. Followed by the 'Forget-Me-Not Waltz.'" He stooped over a bit and looked at Grey. "That was a favorite of your great-great-great-grandmother, they tell me."

Grey thought he must be talking about some relative of Sparky's and didn't pay any attention to his remark. Instead, she watched as the great circle began to turn, and the animals began to move slowly.

"One time around to pick your steed," the stationmaster called. "Pick carefully, very carefully, my friends."

"I shall ride the hare," Sparky announced, trying to sound English again and pointing to a leaping white rabbit draped in garlands of carved roses. It wore a saddle of pink and gold with a necklace and crown of carved golden rope woven with carved roses. Grey admired the huge, furry paws and enormous ears. The rabbit's smile hinted at a secret, and the one blue eye they could see from where they stood shone bright with amusement.

"Which one do you want, Grey?" Sparky urged. "You have to pick. *Now!*"

Grey didn't like to be rushed about making decisions, but she tried to put herself into a decision-making mode. She liked the giraffe, but it didn't move up and down very far. If it did, it would bump its head on the ceiling, she realized. She considered a beautiful wolf, and a swan with jet black eyes, and many horses, each with a flowing wooden mane and real horsehair tail. One jumping black horse caught her eye. It wore a painted tapestry blanket and silver armor, like a knight's horse. Colored banners flew from its gleaming arched neck.

"I think the black horse," she said slowly, but she still

wasn't sure.

"All abooaarrd," the stationmaster called. The carousel slowed to a stop and the girls scrambled up a red-carpeted ramp to the waiting animals.

Sparky climbed on the rabbit immediately. Grey touched its huge front paw as she hurried toward the black horse. The paw felt strangely soft and warm, but it was wood, so she knew that was impossible.

The music grew louder now, and the carousel began to turn faster. Grey almost changed her mind and chose a brown and white spotted horse with Native American decorations just because it sat next to Sparky and the rabbit, but then she hurried on. The black horse waited just ahead and she knew she could still see Sparky if she turned around.

Grey felt a little silly when she found her horse and climbed into the silver saddle with dragons carved along the sides. She was really too old for carousels, she told herself, but her excitement grew as she rode in the dark with nobody else there except Sparky. Her aunt and uncle must have arranged the ride as a special welcome for her, she thought. She decided it was very nice of them. Grey reminded herself to be sure to thank them tomorrow.

The black horse moved forward, a jumper with its front hooves pawing the air. She imagined the shudder of its neck, the way real horses do, but she knew that couldn't be. The horse's head arched back and its teeth bared around the silver bit. Grey could see its glass eyes reflecting the lights as the march blared and the carousel spun. It was a proud horse, and strong. On its bridle the artist had carved the name, Night Music.

"Oh, that's the perfect name for you," she said, leaning forward for balance, but not grabbing the brass pole. She knew that was only there for little kids.

"Thank you," the horse answered without moving its wooden lips over the silver bit. "If you get sleepy, go to the pig."

Grey wasn't sure whether she heard the words or just imagined them. She was very tired, and the march pounded in her ears. Of course, she told herself, she only *thought* she heard the horse speaking amid all the noise. After all, she reasoned, horses don't talk...especially wooden horses.

Grey glanced about. To her left, next to the center, two lions pulled a little cart. The lions wore harnesses of bright red and each one held one foot high, as if dancing. To her right stood the white pig, almost as big as the horse and covered in garlands of carved flowers. It didn't move up and down, but looked into the darkness beyond the carousel as if on guard. Grey especially admired the pig's daffodils, which looked so real, as did the pink roses and crown of white daisies on its head. They all looked so real!

From behind her she heard Sparky yell, "Grey, look!" as thousands of shimmery bubbles filled the air. Some of them popped and some stretched away into the night, wobbling upward toward the moon. And then more came. Grey thought they were very beautiful and let her head fall back to watch them, her arms around the neck of the black horse. But it was so hard to keep her eyes open, and soon she just let them close as she enjoyed the breeze in her hair.

Grey felt her arms slipping from the warm, dark neck. She couldn't keep her eyes open. She remembered the words: If you get sleepy, go to the pig. Good advice, she thought. It looked like a much lower and safer seat. If she didn't move, she'd probably fall and break an arm or something. That would not be a very good start to her new adventures, with her new family, in this new town called Bailey's Chase.

Sliding down from the black horse, she flung herself onto the broad back of the white pig and let her head rest among the flowers. The pig felt warm, she realized. It is a real pig, she thought dreamily, with smooth, stiff white hair and thoughtful maroon eyes. The eyes looked intelligent, like those of a person who reads a lot of books. A pig who would love to hang out in libraries. Grey smiled at the ridiculous thought as the music changed to a waltz, and then she fell asleep.

But the hundred glass eyes in the carousel animals

did not sleep. Not the giraffe's big brown eyes, not the tiger's yellow ones. Not even the ostrich's tan eyes with their droopy, fluttery lids. Not the rabbit's pink eyes, wide above its twitching whiskers as it leaped in the waltz with Sparky on its back. All the animals, warm and breathing as they danced, watched. They watched the brave black horse paw with its hooves at the bubbles.

Sparky watched, too, her eyes wide in wonder. She could see Grey asleep on the white pig that kept looking over its shoulder at Grey like a worried mother. And she could see the armored horse battling the bubbles as the music soared around them.

"Bloody," Sparky whispered as the animals slowly turned to glossy paint and wooden faces again. The music faded to a wheezing sound. The carousel slowed and then stopped completely.

"The Midnight Special is over," the stationmaster announced as the lights flickered out and the oldest Bailey girl came over to lift Grey down from the pig's back.

Sparky grabbed Grey's hand and walked beside her as her father carried her to the waiting van. When Sparky looked over her shoulder, she thought she saw the rabbit wiggle its nose and look at her. And she was pretty sure the pig smiled. Then the carousel went dark again and quiet as a secret.

Walking to the car with her family, Sparky's head spun with the fascinating sights she had just witnessed. She shook her head and blinked her eyes. It was too much to believe. She wondered if she could have possibly been dreaming. No one else seemed to notice anything unusual. Since she knew her family would laugh and remark about her big imagination, she decided to not mention it.

Chapter Two

The next morning Sparky woke up early. She watched the sun spilling from a window across her flowered rug. Rubbing the sleep from her eyes, she suddenly remembered Grey and glanced at her in the other twin bed. Her cousin slept peacefully with her arms wrapped around her pillow.

Being too excited about her new roommate to go back to sleep, Sparky stretched and sat up. For a minute it felt funny having somebody else in her room. I think this might be okay, too, she thought. When she got used to it.

Then she remembered the strange sights she had witnessed while they rode the Midnight Express. Thinking about it, it seemed as weird and puzzling as the night before. Glancing again at the sleeping Grey, Sparky could hardly wait for her to wake up. She was dying to ask her if she remembered anything unusual about the carousel. The stationmaster hadn't seemed to notice anything strange. Her family had been nearby, but they hadn't mentioned anything out of the ordinary. No one but Sparky had seen the wooden creatures turn into real animals, and nobody else had seen the horse battle the bubbles. Maybe it really was just her imagination, she thought with a sigh. Her family had always told her she had a wild imagination. Maybe they were right. Yet, it seemed so real.

It might really be fun to have someone her own age in the house, she decided. She got out of bed and quietly pulled on her T-shirt and shorts. She didn't put her shoes on because Grey was still asleep and Mom had said not to wake her. Carrying her shoes, Sparky tiptoed out of the room and closed the door quietly. She ran downstairs, taking the steps two at a time. She hurried through the front hall and dining room and burst into the kitchen.

"Hi, Mom," she said as she approached her mother, who sat at the big table.

"Well, look who's up early after getting to bed so late last night," her mom said. "Just too excited to sleep with the arrival of your new roommate?"

"I guess so," Sparky admitted. "It does seem funny sharing a room with someone after being by myself for so long."

"You'll get used to it," Mom said. "I always shared a room with my sister, and I think it made us extra close."

"Aunt Becky? Is that why you like to go shopping together?"

"I'm sure that's part of the reason. Anyway," she continued, "I hope you and Grey become as close as Aunt Becky and I."

"Maybe, but I don't even know her yet. That's what seems so strange, I guess."

"She's been through a lot and is making a huge adjustment, you know. I hope you'll give her lots of time to get settled in and used to us and our ways. You know, every family is different."

"I know. She's still asleep," she told her mother. "I tried to be extra quiet like you told me."

Mom sipped coffee from a big brown mug. She reached over and ruffled Sparky's curls fondly. She didn't say anything about sparks.

"I expect she's very tired from the long trip," her mother said. "You can show her where the cereal and juice are when she wakes up. Then you can help her unpack. I think you two had better stay around here today. No running all over town, understand? Maybe you can help me in the shop."

Sparky's mother ran a beauty shop on the glassed-in front porch of their house, a big Victorian house with a huge front porch. The old house and the porch sagged a little toward the yard. When she was little Sparky liked to set pennies on their edges and watch them roll down the sloping floor until they crashed into the wall. The women who came to have their hair done gave her the pennies, and she got to keep them. It was fun then, but it seemed like a pretty dumb thing to do by the time she started the third grade. By then she'd gotten old enough to straighten the magazines and sweep the floor. When she got even older sometimes her mother let her wash somebody's hair on busy days and that was fun. Mostly the shop was boring unless one of the clients forgot about Sparky and started talking about something kids weren't supposed to hear. Then her mother would always say, "Little pitchers have big ears," and send her into the house.

"Grey says I have sparks in my hair." She watched her mother closely for a reaction.

"That sometimes happens when you use a strong shampoo," her mother said. "Come into the shop and I'll massage a little conditioner into it. That will control the static electricity. I wondered when you'd start taking an interest in your hair, honey. Guess you're growing up, huh?" Mom set her coffee cup down and glanced at her watch.

Sparky didn't want to disappoint her mother, but she didn't think 'growing up' had anything to do with the sparks.

"Um, I don't think it's static electricity," she said. "And Grey's eyes change color, too. It's weird."

"I'm sure lots of things seem weird at your age," Mom said with a laugh. "I hope she likes the bike Dad had sent over from the store."

"She will–it's almost exactly like mine. We can take some long rides."

"Well, maybe later, but you and Grey stay around here today. She must be exhausted," her mother repeated as a bell on the porch announced her first client. "This one's a perm," she told Sparky, who hated the ammonia smell of permanent solution. "Stay out of the shop for an hour or two. It upsets everybody when you throw yourself on the floor, clutching your throat and claiming to be a vampire dying from the fumes."

"Well, I think perm solution *could* kill vampires," Sparky said with a mischievous grin. "At least ruin their sense of smell, which could prove fatal."

"Fortunately no vampires have appointments this morning," her mother answered, smiling. "By the way, there's a loaf of raisin bread for you and Grey in the washing machine. I hid it so the others wouldn't eat it all. It's the kind with icing, so don't put it in the toaster."

"Wow, Mom, thanks," Sparky said. Raisin bread was always a treat. Maybe they could toast it on a stick over a cigarette lighter, she thought. There must be about ten thousand of them in her oldest brother's room, but she didn't tell her mother that. She might be a kid sister, but she wasn't a snitch.

"Hey, you're up," she said a few minutes later, after going back upstairs. Grey stood already dressed in shorts and sneakers and a pale yellow polo shirt. Her bags and suitcases sat open, but Sparky could tell she didn't really want to unpack right then.

"Want me to show you around?"

"That would be great," Grey answered as she looked at the room. "It feels kind of funny, being in a strange place, you know? But I like your house. It's a real Victorian, isn't it?"

Sparky didn't see anything special about a Victorian

house. Half the houses in Bailey's Chase were just as old, and all of them had creaky wooden staircases in the front hall. Most had bay windows and big front porches, too. Just old houses.

"I guess so," she said. "But it isn't *haunted* or anything."

"You sound like you wish it *was* haunted," Grey said, grinning.

"I do," Sparky answered. "A ghost would be so awesome!"

Grey's blue eyes looked straight at Sparky. They were changing colors again, all shades of a summer sky. "Awesome...like the carousel last night?" Grey said. "I must have been dreaming, because I thought the black horse said something to me. Isn't that weird?"

Sparky threw herself backward onto her bed, gave a kick, and then sat straight up. "*Yes!* I knew something strange happened. What did he say?" she asked, wide-eyed with interest.

"He said, 'If you get sleepy, go to the pig.' By the way, your hair is doing it again. The sparks."

Sparky ignored the comment about her hair. She was so thrilled that Grey had seen what she'd seen, that she flopped back onto the bed again and laughed.

Grey watched her and waited.

"Something really weird did happen, Grey," Sparky whispered. She rose up on an elbow and looked at her cousin. "When the bubbles started coming really fast, the animals came to *life* and watched. They didn't like it. Then your horse fought the bubbles with his hooves. You were asleep on the pig then. You didn't see, but I did! I thought for a minute I was crazy or something. But you saw it too, so it really did happen."

The two girls looked at each other for a minute. Then Grey said, "Do these strange things happen in Bailey's Chase all the time?"

"Not until last night," Sparky told her, standing on the bed to adjust the circus poster on the wall. "Not until you got here. Until then nothing *ever* happened around here." She turned and looked at Grey. "Hey, maybe you're magic or something!"

"Right," Grey said, laughing. "Except I never was before. And *you're* the one with sparklers for hair!"

"Not until last night, Grey. I never had the sparks until last night, honest! Did your eyes ever change color before?"

"No," Grey said as she looked into a long mirror on the closet door. "But they're changing now, aren't they?" She watched her reflection in amazement.

"Yeah. But my mom didn't see any sparks in my hair this morning. I told her, but she said it was probably static electricity."

"That is not static electricity," Grey said, grinning and touching Sparky's blonde hair. "I wonder if anybody besides us can see your sparks and my eyes changing."

Sparky looked at herself in the mirror, still fascinated

at what she saw. Suddenly she said, "Hey, let's get Newt and see if he notices. He's always doing science stuff and notices everything. If he doesn't see, then we're just imagining it. Come on. He can have some raisin bread with us."

Grey cocked her head. "Who is Newt? And what raisin bread?"

"Newt lives in our carriage house, and the raisin bread's in the washer," Sparky said as if everyone kept bread in washers.

"What's a carriage house?" Grey asked as she brushed her hair.

"Well, it's like this. A long time ago the people who lived in these old houses had horses and carriages." She glanced at Grey. "For transportation, you know. Cars probably weren't even invented yet, or maybe people just weren't used to them. Anyway, no one has horses anymore, so they just use the carriage houses for storage."

"But someone lives in yours?"

"Yeah, Dad made an apartment out of the top of ours, and Newt and his dad live there. It's the upstairs part. The downstairs part is like their garage, except they don't have a car."

"No car?"

"Nope, just a motorcycle. His dad goes everywhere on it. Newt has his own helmet and gets to ride behind him sometimes."

"What if it rains?"

"They wear rain ponchos. If it's really bad weather or if it's an emergency, they call a taxi. That's what they did when Newt had to get his appendix taken out last year."

Grey thought Newt and his father lived a very interesting life.

"Anyway, with no car there's lots of extra room in the garage, so Newt keeps his science stuff there."

"Okay. Now tell me about Newt."

"His real name is Newton and he loves science. He was named for Sir Isaac Newton, who's some famous scientist. Newt's really smart. He's a year older than us."

"And he just lives with his dad?"

"Yep. My dad says his dad is a genius except he drinks too much, and that's why they live in the apartment over our old carriage house instead of a mansion on Harrison Heights. That's the rich part of town. Come on," she said as she tugged on her cousin's hand.

Grey followed her cousin as they clattered down narrow back stairs that smelled of fresh toast and oranges. Then they ran through the kitchen with its big yellow table, and across a back porch, which housed a washer and dryer. Laundry sat stacked in neat piles on the floor.

Sparky sat down on the back steps and put on her sneakers. Grey looked around the back yard. On the far back edge, by the alley, she could see the old carriage house. It was made of round stones and had a peaked roof with a weather vane on top. It looked like a place where Hansel and Gretel might live.

"Hey, Newt," Sparky called as they crossed the backyard and opened the gate. Grey found the carriage house very charming, especially the garden in front where a boy in shorts and a safari hat knelt in the grass. He stared down at something with a magnifying glass. The safari hat had badges and buttons all over it, and the boy had freckles and sunburn all over him.

"Hey, Newt," Sparky said again. "This is my cousin Grey. We want you to look at us and see if you see anything weird."

"Hi, Grey," he said without looking up. "I heard you were coming. Welcome to Bailey's Chase. Want to see about a thousand springtails?"

Grey had no idea what a springtail was, but she said, "Sure," and leaned forward to look.

Sparky rolled her brown eyes and made a face. "Bugs," she told Grey. "He's been doing bugs all summer. Not even regular ones like moths. Before that it was rocks and before that clams or something."

"Mussels, not clams," Newt said, standing up and brushing off his knees. "I studied mussels, quite different actually. So what am I supposed to look at?"

"Us," Grey said. "My eyes, Sparky's hair. So what do you see?" They lined up and watched him closely for a reaction.

He gave them a quick glance. "Just two girls," he said as if nothing could be more boring. "Now springtails—there's something really interesting. They're as small as fleas but they don't bite, and they've got this thing like a mousetrap spring built onto them. When something's after them they just release the spring and it's like a pogo stick. It throws them as far as a hundred meters!"

Grey could tell he was really excited about the insects. She and Sparky exchanged a knowing glance. *He didn't see!*

"Bugs, big deal," Sparky said. "You want some raisin bread? Mom left us a whole loaf in the washer."

"I'll look at the springtails," Grey said. She took the magnifying glass from Newt's hand and knelt in the garden. Sure enough, lots of tiny insects crawled around on the damp dirt.

"Shouldn't you kill them so they won't ruin your garden?" she asked.

"Oh, no," he answered, as if she'd suggested mass murder. "Springtails recycle a lot of stuff. They're good for the soil."

"Well, okay," Grey replied. There didn't seem to be anything else to say about the bugs. She wondered if any of them had hopped into her socks with their pogo sticks. Also, she wondered why Newt hadn't seen the sparks and her changing eyes. Grey read a lot of books, but she knew the difference between made-up things and real ones. Sparky's fiery hair and her own changing blue eyes were real, so why didn't this boy see them, too? *Very puzzling.*

They tromped back to the house and Sparky got the raisin bread out of the washer. "We can't put it in the toaster," she said. "It's got icing on the top. One of my sisters did that, twice, and both times the icing melted and caught on fire. Mom said we didn't have toasters in the house for a long time after that, but I don't remember. I wasn't even born. All the good stuff happened before I was born, I guess."

"We can toast it outside," Newt said, his pea green eyes bright as if he'd just invented something. "Like the Gypsies! I'll make a fire in a shallow hole, and then when it dies down to coals--"

"What Gypsies?" Sparky said. "How do you know anything about how Gypsies cook?"

"Oh," he said, taking off his hat and running slender fingers through his bristly red hair. "Didn't you hear? Some Gypsies came to town last night. Real ones. They've got a van painted with all kinds of designs and a flag with a red wheel on it. They're camped on the river down by the station. I saw them. The guys and I went down there last night. Actually, they're camped at the old ghost town!"

While Newt went off to build a fire, Sparky and Grey had some orange juice and cereal at the big yellow table. They found it interesting that the Gypsies came to town on the same night Grey arrived. In a town where nothing interesting ever happened, two major events had happened at the same time.

"The ghost town's just some old shacks on the river where people lived a long time ago before my mom and dad were born," Sparky said. "The people used to get mussels from the river and make buttons out of the shells. Then somebody invented plastic buttons and nobody wanted shell buttons anymore, so they went away to do some other kind of work, I guess. Now all their places are empty and full of weeds. Some of the people down there a long time ago were Gypsies, too. That's what people say."

"Wow," Grey said. "I've never seen a ghost town. Can we go see it? And the Gypsies?"

Sparky wanted to go, but remembered what her mother had said.

"Mom wants us to stay around here today. She thinks you're probably all tired out from your long trip."

Grey nodded. "Your mom seems really nice. But I'm not tired. Do you think if we asked her...?"

"She's doing a perm right now," Sparky said. "Believe me, you don't want to go in there." Sparky clutched her throat with both hands. "*Arrrrgggh!*"

Grey laughed.

"We'll go hang out in the shop later. Maybe she'll see how not tired you are and we can take off! But don't mention the Gypsies; that will freak her out."

"Got it," Grey agreed.

It took forever for Newt to get the coals just right in the little fire he built with sticks in a hole near his garden, but it worked fine. They toasted the bread on sharp sticks, keeping the edges up so the icing wouldn't catch on fire. Grey had three slices and thought the morning was wonderful.

"We got to ride the carousel last night," she told Newt. "At midnight."

She could see it impressed him, but he quickly hid it. "That's for kids," he said. "I'm eleven now."

Grey thought he seemed a little sad about being eleven and not being allowed to ride anymore.

"It was creepy when the bubbles came," Sparky told him. "The animals didn't like it, and the black horse, Night Music, stomped the bubbles."

"Oh, sure," he said, shaking his head in disbelief. "Like that could really happen. A wooden horse on a pole can't stomp anything, and bubbles reflect like glass does. Maybe a *kid* would see something reflected on the surface of a soap bubble and find it scary. You probably stayed up past your bedtime, is what I think."

Grey watched Sparky to see if she'd get angry, but she didn't. She wiped her sticky fingers on the sides of her red T-shirt with zebras on the front and said with a shrug, "I knew you'd say that. But it happened whether you believe it or not." She glanced at Grey, who nodded in agreement.

Later, Sparky and Grey spent a great deal of time putting Grey's things away in a big white chest of drawers Sparky's dad had brought down from the attic. Socks and underwear in the top left drawer, T-shirts in the top right. Then pants and shorts in the next drawer, and winter clothes in the bottom two. Grey carefully folded everything just so. Sparky hoped her mom wouldn't expect her to be as neat as Grey.

Sparky pushed her clothes to one side of the closet to make room for Grey's clothes. Grey noticed a shiny brown door with a white china knob on the back wall of the closet, but was too busy to ask about it. She carefully hung her dresses and skirts and her black winter coat with braided knots for buttons beside Sparky's clothes. Sparky thought she had never seen so many beautiful clothes in her life. "That's sure a fancy coat," she said.

"It's for going to the theater and concerts and stuff," Grey said.

"We don't go to many theaters and concerts," Sparky told her. "But we do go to church and sometimes to a wedding or a funeral. I guess you could wear it then." Then she added, "Oh, we go to movies sometimes, but we don't get dressed up for them."

Finally the closet was full. Grey had officially moved in.

"Why is there a door in the back of the closet?" Grey asked.

"It goes to the attic," Sparky explained. "In the old days houses didn't have closets. Somebody put closets in this house later. They just built the closet over that door. Nobody ever uses it. There's another door to the attic in the hall. That's the one we use mostly."

"Very interesting," Grey said, thinking a hidden door in a closet would be convenient if you needed to hide.

Sort of like a secret passageway. She made a mental note to use the hidden door in a book she would write some day.

After putting away all the clothes, they lined Grey's shoes up beside Sparky's on the closet floor. Then the girls made their beds and put the luggage into the hall. "Dad'll take it to the attic later," Sparky said.

"I *really* like this house," Grey told Sparky as a piercing whistle came from outside.

"That's Newt," said Sparky. "He whistles like that when there's something interesting going on, or at least when he *thinks* it's interesting." She rolled her eyes. "Probably he's discovered more bugs."

Grey followed as Sparky led the way down the stairs and into the backyard. Newt balanced on his knees peering into some shrubbery. "What's going on?" Grey asked when they reached Newt's side.

"It's a rabbit and it's hurt," Newt said as he crawled along the shrubs trying to spot the hiding animal. "I saw it cross the yard and it was limping–real bad."

"What do you think happened to it?" Sparky asked as she knelt down beside Newt.

"I don't know, but if we can catch it, maybe we can help."

"How can we do that?" Grey asked.

Newt straightened up and ran his fingers through his hair, as if that would help him think. "You girls stand over there," he said, gesturing as he spoke, "and I'll scare it out of the bushes and make it run toward you."

"We can't catch a wild rabbit with our bare hands," Sparky said.

"You're right," Newt said. "Let me think. I know," he said quickly. "I think there's some fishing net in the garage, seining net like you stretch across a creek or a pond. I'll go try to find it. Then you can hold the net between you, and I'll drive the rabbit into it. That should work. I've seen zoologists on television catch wild animals like that. Be right back!" Newt turned and trotted off toward the garage.

"Let's try to find it," Sparky said, dropping to her knees.

The girls crawled around in the grass peering into the bushes for a glimpse of the rabbit. Sparky reached forward and rustled the dry leaves under the bushes with her hands. The noise caused the quivering rabbit to move a few feet along the foundation of the house.

"I see it," Grey whispered. "It's just a baby rabbit."

"Yeah, I see it," Sparky said. "It looks scared."

The girls talked to the rabbit, making sounds that children make when they talk to babies or puppies or kittens. Singsong sounds in words that don't really have to make any sense.

"Come on, bunny, it's all right," Grey sang.

"You can come to us; we won't hurt you," Sparky added.

The rabbit didn't move, but twitched its pink nose as

if it heard them. It looked at the girls with eyes black as midnight. Grey felt herself sliding into the blackness of those eyes as Sparky sang, "Bunny, bunny," over and over like a chant. She stared into the rabbit's black eyes as well, and tried hard not to blink.

"Bunny, bunny," Grey whispered, her words like soft shadows of Sparky's, each word echoing, their two voices as one in the dim light under the shrubs. With little, jerky movements the small rabbit began to hop toward them.

"Bunny, bunny, it's okay," Sparky whispered, trying to keep the excitement she felt out of her voice.

"Okay, okay." Grey echoed softly.

As the girls stretched flat on the grass, the tiny rabbit hopped right between their outstretched hands. Very softly they touched it with one finger each, making no attempt to grab it for fear of scaring it away. After stroking its head and back for a minute or so while its nose twitched, they gently moved it toward them and away from the shrubbery.

"Be careful," Grey warned quietly, as Sparky scooped the animal into her arms and stood up, cradling it like a puppy.

The rabbit lay quietly making no attempt to escape as the girls continued to pet it. Then Grey noticed something shiny.

"Look," she said, pointing to one of its back paws. "That's why it's limping."

Sparky bent her head to look as Grey touched a piece

of wire twisted around the furry paw. It was a spiral of wire, like the wire that binds a school notebook. Very gently Grey loosened the wire and removed it as the rabbit lay peacefully in Sparky's arms.

"There, you should be fine now," Grey told the rabbit.

For a few quiet seconds, the black eyes stared into the girls' eyes with a look that made them feel a little dizzy. "Thank you," the look said. They could almost hear it. Then, very gently, Sparky set the rabbit down in the grass and the cousins watched it hop away, no longer limping. The girls were very pleased with themselves for being able to help, but at the same time somewhat amazed.

Newt returned from the garage, his arms filled with wadded-up fishing net. "I finally found it," he reported.

"We don't need it anymore," Sparky said. "We caught the rabbit. It had a piece of wire stuck on its foot."

"And we took it off," Grey added happily.

Newt dropped the grungy netting on the grass. "How did you catch it?" he asked in disbelief.

The girls looked at each other, still somewhat puzzled by the experience. Finally, Sparky said, "We don't know– it was odd. We just talked to it and it came to us." Grey nodded.

Newt looked skeptical as he asked, "Didn't it bite or scratch or anything?"

"No," Grey answered. "It was very peaceful." She hesitated a moment, and then added, "Kinda like magic. It heard and understood us–like magic," she whispered. Sparky watched her thoughtfully.

"Yeah, right." Newt scowled. "You girls and your kid games." After a moment he told them, "Actually, that's very odd behavior for a wild animal. It must have been sick. I hope it didn't have rabies or something." After thinking about it for a second, he offered, "Frankly, I don't think rabbits get rabies; now if it had been a skunk--" His voice trailed off as he returned to the garage carrying the netting.

The two cousins weren't thinking about rabies or skunks. They stared at each other, thinking about the way it felt when they sang to the rabbit and looked into its black eyes. That wasn't anything usual and they knew it. *What was going on?* They both wondered.

Chapter Three

The girls went back into the house and up to their bedroom. The open windows allowed the morning breeze to ruffle the sheer curtains. Sparky and Grey sat on their beds facing each other, still trying to make sense of the strange events that had been happening to them. Things that had never happened before–to either of them. They were completely baffled.

"What's going on?" asked a bewildered Grey, who always wanted to understand things. "Newt didn't see your sparks or my eyes changing, and then the rabbit…well, that was certainly strange. It acted like it understood us."

"Gosh, I don't know," Sparky answered slowly. "But something weird is going on, that's for sure–that's for bloody sure."

"Maybe we should talk to your mother and try to explain things."

"No way. She'd just tell Dad and he'd decide we'd been watching too much TV and start limiting our TV time. And they'd *never* let us watch any more scary movies."

"So we just keep it a secret, right? At least until we

figure it all out."

"Right," Sparky said. Then she suddenly added, "Want to take a blood oath?"

"I don't think so," Grey replied cautiously.

"Then let's both say, 'Scouts' Honor,' at the same time," Sparky suggested.

Grey agreed and the girls repeated the words as they held three fingers to their foreheads, making the Girl Scout pledge.

"I wonder," Grey said, almost to herself, "if any other animals would act like they could understand us. Do you have any pets?"

"Just a cat."

"Could we try it on your cat?"

"Marmalade? She's probably out running around somewhere, and besides that, she's so contrary, she'd probably act like she didn't hear us even if she did. She only checks in when she's hungry."

"You don't have any other pets?"

"Just some goldfish, in the aquarium in the front hall."

"Let's try it on *them*," Grey suggested.

"Goldfish? I don't know–they seem pretty stupid."

"It's worth a try! Come on."

The girls bounded off their beds and down the stairway to the open front hall. The fish tank sat on a stand near the bottom of the stairs. Several fat goldfish swam through the ferny green plants, as if crossing layers of busy streets only they could see.

"Now, how do you talk to goldfish?" Sparky giggled, as the girls leaned down and peered into the aquarium. Green plants swayed in the water. Bubbles floated up through the water as the filter did its work.

"Just like we talked to the rabbit," Grey responded thoughtfully. Then she started making soft sounds and gentle pleas to the fish, but the fish continued to swim in erratic patterns through the brightly lit waters and didn't seem to notice at all.

"It's not working," Sparky said. "Try saying something else."

When more of Grey's efforts were ignored, she said, "They don't even know I'm here."

"Gee," Sparky conceded, "maybe it really *was* just a sick rabbit, after all."

"Something's not right. Maybe it just works on mammals."

"Or maybe just on rabbits."

"Or maybe not at all," Grey said. "Sparky, I have an idea! Maybe we *both* have to do it!"

"You want *me* to try?"

"No, I mean maybe we *both* have to do it at the same time!"

"Yeah, let's try that!"

Soon both girls crouched in front of the fish tank, noses pressed to the glass, staring into the waters.

"Hey, fishy, fishy, fishy," they said, followed by,

"come on, little fishes; we want to talk to you." And then, "Listen to us, goldfish, we are trying to communicate with you!"

The girls giggled at their own efforts because they felt so foolish talking to goldfish. Alternately, they checked over their shoulders to make sure that no one could see or hear them. They knew they would never hear the last of it, if one of the older kids or Newt walked into the room. But Newt never came into the house without an invitation, and the older kids all had summer jobs until school started. Mom worked in the shop, and of course, Dad was *always* at his store during the day. Feeling safe, they continued to talk earnestly to the fish, urging them to cooperate, their words making a soft chant in the silent hall.

Then suddenly, and unexpectedly, the fish stopped swimming in circles and lined up in a single file row facing the glass! Six goldfish hung almost completely still facing the girls. The only movement among them was the constant flutter of fins as the fish held their positions. The girls gasped, but continued talking softly to the fish. To an outsider, it would have been hard to say whose eyes opened wider, or whose mouths hung open further, the fish or the girls. Everything stilled. It was weird and it was really happening.

Finally, the girls could stand it no longer and abandoned the test. The fish moved away, their orange tails swaying, going back to the business of being ordinary goldfish. It had actually worked, this power or ability or whatever. Momentarily overwhelmed with their success, they dropped onto the rug and faced each other. They laughed and cheered and slapped hands together, triumphantly giving each other high-fives.

"I can't believe it," Sparky said with a gasp. "Could they *hear* us–did we have *control* over them? This is so unreal."

Grey's eyes widened. She said softly, "But it only worked when we did it *together*! That must mean something."

"Like we can only talk to animals if we do it together?"

"Maybe more than that, Sparky. Maybe there are other things we could do if we both concentrated on it."

"Like what? Like *magic*?"

"I don't know. Let's try some stuff and see if anything else works."

The notion of magical powers immediately intrigued Sparky. She grabbed her cousin's hand and gave her a tug. "Come on, back up to our room!"

Once in the room, Sparky closed the door, threw herself against it, and faced Grey. "Okay, now what?" She trembled with excitement.

"I don't know–let me think," Grey replied as she paced the room, hands to her face in thought. After a few seconds, she said, "I saw a movie once about a man who could make things move by just staring at them. Let's try that."

Sparky pointed to a plant growing in a clay pot on the windowsill. "The African violet," she urged.

Both girls stared at the flower, but nothing happened. Then Grey said, "Let's both stare for exactly one minute and don't say anything, but think real hard M-O-V-E."

"If we can't look at the clock, how can we tell when a minute is over?"

"Just guess," Grey said. Then as the thought struck her she said, "Let's hold hands. When we squeeze hands we'll both stop."

So the two girls stood in front of the plant for a lengthy period of time conducting their experiment. Just when their eyes began to tire and they were both ready to stop, the plant trembled slightly.

"I saw it! It moved," Sparky almost yelled.

"It could have been the wind moving it," Grey decided. Then she moved the plant to the top of the dresser and they tried again. Amazingly, it worked again. The excited girls conducted variations of their experiment by standing farther away and for shorter time periods. It seemed that the plant always moved slightly, no matter how they changed the situation. But when just one girl tried, nothing happened. For some unknown reason, they had to do it together. They were sure about that. The girls giggled, jubilant that they could do this and decided to try to move something else.

"Let's try with something non-living," Grey

suggested, sounding very much like a scientist.

"How about that shoe?" Sparky said, pointing to one of Grey's black dance slippers on the floor near the closet.

Again, with combined efforts, the girls could cause the shoe to tremble slightly. No big or dramatic movements, just a slight tremor, and only with their combined focus and concentration. Dazzled by their success, they looked for something else to test.

"Let's focus on the circus poster over my bed," Sparky said. "Let's see what we can do with that. This will be a real test, because it's thumb-tacked to the wall. Surely it can't move."

The girls stared at the poster of an elephant against a background of red. The elephant wore a sparkling blanket and had one foot on a stool painted with stars. Its head bent back as if singing, and its trunk made a letter J. Once more, the girls concentrated as hard as they could–lips pressed firmly together, eyes focused, unblinking, on the elephant. But the poster didn't move. Instead, something even more spectacular happened: the elephant in the poster turned its head and looked at them. It turned very slowly and not very far, but the huge head did move. They could see the paper eyes sparkling with amusement as the paper trunk snorted softly. Then it all changed back and the elephant froze in the position it had always held. Just a picture, locked forever in time. The girls looked at each other with breathless awe-struck expressions.

"Wow," said Sparky. She squealed and jumped

excitedly on the bed. "I don't believe it!" She threw both arms over her head and fell over backwards onto the soft covers.

"This is impossible," said Grey softly as Sparky continued to bounce around. "That's an old circus poster from a long time ago. The elephant in the picture can't still be alive. The real one, I mean. But the picture is. It moved. It looked at us!" Grey felt dizzy, the way she always felt when she didn't understand something.

"It's not alive. It has to be just an illusion," Sparky said, seeing Grey's eyes turning darker and darker blue. "We just made an illusion, that's all. I don't know how, but I think it's bloody neat!"

Grey watched the elephant curiously and didn't say anything. Her mind swirled with too much to think about.

Finally, when the cousins could think of nothing else to test, and they had almost exhausted themselves with the effort, they decided to call it quits for the day. They didn't understand their power, or where it had come from, or why it had just started, but they were amazed and delighted with the whole business. They reminded each other of their vow of silence and promised to keep working on their newly-found powers, hoping to enlarge them with experience.

After lunch, they lay on their beds and talked softly about everything except magic. Grey shared information about her journey and bits of her life before she came to Bailey's Chase. Sparky told her about the neighborhood and the school, especially about her favorite teachers.

"What's your favorite color?" Sparky asked.

"Blue, what's yours?"

"Red. What's your favorite movie?"

"The Wizard of Oz. What's yours?"

"The Parent Trap."

"I loved that, too."

"I bet my favorite sandwich is the weirdest one you ever heard of," Sparky said.

"Try me. Mine's pretty weird too."

"Brace yourself," Sparky said. "Everyone thinks it's so gross except me and I love it."

"Tell me."

"Okay, well you know how everyone loves peanut butter and everyone loves sliced tomatoes?" She paused a moment. "I guess I'm the only person in the world who likes peanut butter and tomato sandwiches."

Grey giggled. "That is unusual. Mine's rather strange too. I like corned beef with grape jelly. I don't know why everyone thinks that's so crazy; we always put mint jelly on roast lamb."

"It sounds pretty awful to me, but if you like it, that makes it okay. I'll ask Mom to buy some corned beef for you. We always have grape jelly; it's my favorite."

Later, they started to play a game, but then decided it was too hot to stay upstairs. "Come on," Sparky suggested. "Let's go down to the beauty shop–it's air-conditioned."

"Good idea. I've been wanting to see it," Grey said, and she followed Sparky down to the shop on the front porch.

After being introduced to her aunt's clients, Grey and Sparky sat on the floor and looked at hairstyles in magazines. Each one chose a grown-up style she hoped to wear someday. Sparky liked the simple bob, while Grey admired the more sophisticated styles. Sparky wondered if that's how ladies who went to theater and concerts wore their hair.

One of the women complained loudly about having a birthday cake stolen from her car in the supermarket parking lot that very morning.

"I left the windows down so the icing wouldn't melt in the heat," the woman said. "I needed to run into the drugstore to pick up a prescription, so I left the car parked and ran next door to the drugstore. In that short time, somebody stole my Betsy's birthday cake! Can you believe the nerve? Probably one of those filthy Gypsies that came to town last night. They steal, you know," she said, with a nod as if stating a fact you might find in an encyclopedia.

"Even worse than that," she continued, "I heard they marry their girls off before they're even fourteen! Can you believe it? Younger than fourteen with some man--"

"Whoops, I think you're ready to rinse," Sparky's mother interrupted, turning on the water in a sink so it made a lot of noise. "Girls, it's so hot, why don't you run downtown for an ice cream cone? I've got a meeting tonight and Dad's cooking, so dinner will be very late. Take your time."

After counting out the right amount of money from Mom's cash box, the girls hopped on their bikes and headed downtown. Soon they stood outside the drugstore licking their ice cream cones.

"Want to go see the Gypsies?" Sparky asked suddenly, catching a drop of chocolate ice cream with the end of her tongue just before it landed on her shirt.

"Sure," Grey said compliantly. "I'm always up for an adventure."

With no thought at all about staying close to home, the girls finished the ice cream cones, mounted their bikes, and headed for the Gypsy camp by the river.

Chapter Four

In less than ten minutes, Grey and Sparky lay sprawled on their stomachs in the high grass of the levee overlooking the river. The grass felt scratchy, but neither of them cared. Just below, in a grove of cottonwood trees, lay the old ghost town. The big building, where people once made shell buttons, and the sagging shacks near it were all falling apart. Even in the cloudy afternoon light the place appeared scary, like it might actually be inhabited by ghosts.

Even stranger than the old buildings with broken windows was a bright lavender van with designs painted on it in dark green and yellow and red. A flag attached to the van rippled in the breeze. The girls had never seen such a flag. The top half was blue and the bottom half green, with a sixteen-spoked red wheel in the middle. The van sat in cottonwood shadows like a bright toy. Everything was quiet. Nobody seemed to be around.

"Wow," Grey whispered. "It's just like Newt said, but I don't see any Gypsies."

Sparky dug her chin into the grass and narrowed her eyes. "I don't think anybody's there," she said. "But that's got to be a Gypsy van. I wonder what it looks like on the inside." She glanced over at her cousin. "Let's sneak down and peek in the windows."

Grey looked up and down the river. Far to their right sat the station. She could hear music from the carousel drifting downstream, but there was nobody on the riverbank. To their left, just beyond the ghost town, a thicket grew right to the water's edge. So there wasn't anybody there, either. Nothing under the quiet, cloudy sky but Grey and Sparky, and a Gypsy van.

"Sure," Grey answered. She got up and followed her cousin down the levee. They sneaked through the tall grass, quietly moving to the clearing by the river. Then slipping from tree to tree, as they had seen Indians do in movies, they edged toward the mysterious Gypsy van. The windows on their side appeared to be covered, so they motioned to each other, agreeing silently to move around behind the van, to check out the windows on the other side.

Reaching the back of the van, they stopped. There on the bank by the river stood a woman, staring at the water, her back to them. The girls froze in place, not certain what to do, sure she had not seen them. Her long white hair covered most of her back and she wore layers of brightly colored skirts. This person, the girls thought, as they glanced at each other with raised eyebrows, must be a real Gypsy.

While the girls tried to decide whether to sneak away or not, the woman's voice rang out, "So you've come."

The girls gasped but didn't move.

Slowly the woman turned and faced the girls. Her smile revealed even white teeth and made wrinkles all over her face. Her black eyes sparkled in the shadows. "So you've come," she repeated. "I've been expecting you. My name is Rupa."

The girls stared at the strange woman with the billowy sleeves and rows of gold chains and necklaces. Even her wrists jangled with bracelets.

"It's…it's very nice to meet you," Grey stammered, trying to be polite.

"Are you a real Gypsy?" Sparky asked quickly.

Rupa frowned slightly. "'Gypsy' is a silly word," she said in a disgusted voice. "A thousand years ago some Europeans thought our people came from Egypt, so they called them 'Gypsies', but we did *not* come from Egypt. We came from India and we are the Roma. Some say Romani, but that doesn't matter. What matters is that you know the truth."

"The truth that you're *not* Gypsies?" Grey asked.

Rupa's eyes grew wide and so did her smile. "Any truth is better than error," she pointed out. As she started walking toward the van, she added, "But there's another truth I've come to tell you. Please follow me."

"What do you mean, you've come to tell us?" Sparky asked, her hands on her hips. "You don't even *know* us."

The old woman stopped walking and faced Sparky.

She stayed silent for a moment, then spoke slowly. "I know why light dances in your curls, little one." Then she turned and pointed her finger at Grey. "And I know why your eyes change color like the blues in a thousand paintings."

The girls stood in silence, dazzled with this Gypsy woman before them.

"You see, I knew your ancestor. People called her Granny Bailey, and she was very old when I was just a little girl. She saved my life. Now I've come to meet you. You must come inside–there's little time."

"What ancestor?" Grey asked. She could smell something delicious inside the van. "And who did you come to meet? Me or Sparky?"

"Both," Rupa said mysteriously. She turned and stepped into the van.

The girls looked at each other. They had been taught never to go anywhere with a stranger. But this wasn't going anywhere, exactly, they reasoned.

"She knows about your hair and my eyes, and she's going to explain it to us," whispered Grey, who could never resist finding answers to questions.

"I think she's nice," added Sparky, who liked almost everybody. "Let's go in."

Rupa waited for them at a small table that folded out of a wall. She motioned for them to come in. She pointed to a man sitting in the back of the van. A red scarf covered most of his hair and a gold earring in one ear glinted in the light. "That's Stefan; he's my driver." The girls looked at the sun-darkened man, who said nothing, but smiled and nodded. Rupa said, "Please sit."

The cousins sat down at the small table facing the mysterious woman. A candle flickered on the table beside some large cards arranged facedown in a stack. Rupa reached behind her for three red cups and a coffeepot. She placed them on the table. She'd already half-filled two of the cups with milk.

"Roma coffee is very strong and sweet," she told them as she filled their cups. "That's why yours will be half milk." She slid a cup of coffee in front of each girl. "Now, there are things you need to know. Watch carefully, I will show you a story."

Sparky sipped her coffee and tried not to make a face. Grey stirred hers with a tiny spoon and tasted it. Surprisingly, she found she liked it. This must have been the aroma that had drifted from the door of the painted van, this sweet coffee. Grey decided she would start drinking coffee as soon as she turned eleven.

"You see these cards," Rupa began, picking up the deck.

"Are they fortune-telling cards?" Sparky asked. "I've heard that Gypsies…er, the Roma people, tell fortunes."

"Some do," Rupa answered. "But never for other Roma. That is forbidden."

"Why is it forbidden?" Grey asked, curious about people who could tell fortunes.

Rupa smiled and her face broke into a thousand wrinkles lit by the candle's flame. "Asking questions is good," she told them. "But getting true answers requires a long time. Watch carefully now. Look and learn."

She turned over one of the big cards. It made a soft whooshing sound on the table. Grey and Sparky looked at each other in surprise and then stared at the card with its strange design. It wasn't a regular playing card like they were used to, with hearts and spades and clubs and diamonds. Instead, it had a picture of a small cabin at the edge of a thick forest. While they watched, they noticed smoke coming from the cabin's chimney, and the smoke actually *moved*!

Sparky blinked. She thought she had surely imagined it, until she heard Grey take a deep breath.

"The card is like a TV or a computer monitor, isn't it?" Grey asked, thinking she had figured it out. "It's showing a film or a tape."

"*Shh*, just watch," Rupa murmured, keeping her eyes down.

As the girls watched the scene, a barefoot little girl with black hair ran to the cabin door, crying. "Help! They're going to get me." She spoke in the same accent as Rupa. "Help me!"

Sparky and Grey could hear pounding footsteps and people shouting. They sounded furious. They saw an old woman open the cabin door. She wore a long old-fashioned print dress and blue apron. Her wild white hair flew with sparks, and her blue eyes changed hue from a summer sky to the darkest winter night.

"Come inside," she told the frightened girl. She closed the door behind the girl and stood in front of it as the angry people arrived. She stood with her arms crossed over her chest. One of the men carried a shovel and waved it in the air. Another held a pitchfork. Some of the others clutched rocks in their hands.

"Those dirty Gypsies stole my horse," said the angry man with the shovel. "I'll show *them!*"

"And that Gypsy girl," a woman announced. "She made my baby sick. They're evil, those Gypsies. Now give us the girl! We demand it!"

"Your horse is in your neighbor's field," the old woman calmly told the man with the shovel. "He kicked through the fence because he was hungry and he saw grass. You need to feed him properly and he'll stay at home."

The crowd became quiet and looked at the man. Leaning on his shovel, he hung his head in shame.

"Your baby is sick because you don't bathe her often enough," she told the woman. "Go home and wash the child in a tub of warm water every day. She'll be fine." At once the woman bit her lip and stared at the ground, her fingers closed tightly around a rock.

The crowd didn't show any intention of leaving. They mumbled angrily to each other.

"Granny Bailey, get out of our way," a big red-faced

man yelled. "We're going to take that Gypsy girl *now*!"

The old woman didn't budge from her position in front of the door. Her white hair flashed and sparkled like fireworks, and her eyes changed from blue to blue-green to almost black.

"No, you're not," she said as she pointed a bony finger at them. As Grey and Sparky watched, hardly able to believe their eyes, the people started instantly changing. One man shrank down becoming a mouse. Another sprouted wings and a beak and became a canary. The man with the shovel dropped it on his foot and howled; only his foot had turned into a paw and his howl a cat's howl. The woman with the sick baby shrieked as she turned into a skunk with two white stripes down its back. They all tried to talk, but found they could no longer understand each other. Everyone waved their paws frantically and babbled, their eyes wide with fear and shock. Soon they crept away, confused and alone. As they left, the girls could see them gradually turn back into real people. Then the card faded to colored swirls and went dark.

"Wow," Sparky said excitedly. "That was neat! What is that thing? Is it some kind of computer or DVD player?" She leaned forward for a closer look.

"Who is Granny Bailey?" Grey asked softly. "And what happened to the little girl?"

"You ask questions, but you don't look around you," Rupa told them. "Look for the answers to your own questions–don't expect to be told. No one else can answer your questions for you. That you must do for yourselves. *Look!*"

Clouds thickened in the sky, making it darker in the van. In the candlelight Grey looked at Sparky and saw light shooting from her hair, just like Granny Bailey's hair. Sparky looked at Grey and saw her eyes change from pale blue to sea blue to a deep, royal blue, just like Granny Bailey's eyes. Both girls looked at Rupa. Inside her white hair they saw the jet-black color it had once been. Behind the wrinkles of her face they saw the face of the young Gypsy girl.

"That was you," Grey declared. "Those people were after you!"

"I get it! Granny Bailey is like us somehow," Sparky added. "Or we're like her. Grey has eyes like hers. And I have the same sparks in my hair!"

Rupa nodded and smiled. "Very good. You have done well, little ones," she said. "You looked for your own answers and you found them. Be proud of yourselves–and your heritage. You see, Granny Bailey was your great-great-great-grandmother."

"She saved your life from those nasty people," Sparky went on. "But how do you know us? How did you know that we would come here today?"

"I can only tell you what I know," Rupa continued. "Since your birth, you have each held something within you that came from your great ancestor. However, it is of no use to you alone. At last, through time and tragedy, the two halves of Granny Bailey's special gift are finally together again. This gift will give you great power. Remember my words: You must learn to use it alone, telling no one. Know this: If you tell, you will lose it. You must do your work in secret." She paused and sipped her coffee. The girls waited anxiously for her to continue.

She set her cup down and placed her hands over the girls' hands. In a soft, knowing voice she said, "There will always be evil in the world, and those who do evil will always be enemies of those who do good. You must use your gift to help others—to make the world a better place, as Granny Bailey did. It must never be used as a toy."

The girls glanced at each other guiltily, remembering how they'd made the shoe tremble just for fun. They squirmed slightly in their seats and gulped, wondering if Rupa knew about that too. Although they were excited about meeting the Gypsy woman and thrilled about the powers she mentioned, they didn't like the sound of enemies lurking around them. For a few moments, they sat in heavy silence, watching the flickering candle, and trying to understand what Rupa had told them.

"Will people try to hurt us because we have this power?" Grey asked quietly.

"And how will they know if we never tell anyone?" Sparky wondered aloud.

"They will know. There have always been evil forces in the world, and they sense when a good power is near them. They will cause problems for you, I promise."

"What should we do?" Grey asked, while Sparky watched, wide-eyed about the whole matter.

"When the time comes, you will know. You have inherited a great and wonderful gift. Do not take it lightly, but do not be afraid." The Gypsy woman's eyes suddenly shone with kindness as she spoke. "I have brought you something that will help to protect you."

Grey and Sparky watched as Rupa took a carved wooden box from a shelf and placed it on the table. Etchings of spirited horses decorated every surface. Grey reached to touch one that reminded her of the black horse on the carousel.

"*Balual, grast*," Rupa said softly. "Wind, horse, the windhorse. He is the guardian of the Roma people, who for a thousand years have wandered with the wind. Because your ancestor saved me, he will watch over you when he can, just as he did last night." The girls glanced at each other, amazed that Rupa knew about the black horse.

She opened the box. Inside, on the black velvet lining, lay two earrings made of the pearly inside surface of a shell. They seemed to glow against the black velvet.

"Your great-great-great grandmother wore these. Just before she died, she gave them to me. Now they are yours." She gently placed them into the girls' hands.

Sparky carefully touched the one in her hand. It was smooth and cool. "They're for pierced ears," she said.

"Mom won't let us get our ears pierced, I can tell you that. Not until we're thirteen."

Grey just stared at the earring in her hand. "What do we do with them?" she asked. "How will they protect us?"

"I don't know," Rupa answered, her dark eyes somber. "Like all good questions, you must answer that for yourselves. Now, I'm afraid we must go. My driver is anxious, and the road is long ahead of us. The rest of our group has already started the journey."

"Thank you, Rupa," Sparky said thoughtfully, suddenly remembering her manners. "It was nice of you to come so far to see us–and to bring us the earrings."

"And to tell us the truth," Grey added. "Thank you, Rupa. Will we see you again? What if…if we need you?" Her voice trembled as she waited for more information.

"You will not see me again," Rupa answered, pulling a black silk scarf around her shoulders. She opened the door for them. "And you will not need me–you have the power. Use it well. Good-bye Grey and Sparky. I leave the goodness of your ancestor with you. Be brave and remember to tell no one!"

In a very little while, the van with the flag on its side was tightly secured, and the driver drove Rupa away. Holding hands and clutching the earrings, the girls stood on the riverbank and watched the van until it disappeared from sight.

Chapter Five

Sparky and Grey told no one of their encounter with Rupa. Nervously, they clutched hands in their room that night, recalling the strange visit. They touched the pearly earrings and wondered about the Gypsy woman's words and warnings. They remembered the admonition to be brave and to use their power for good.

The next day Newt found them some nylon fishing line, and each girl carefully cut a piece, tied an earring to it, and hung it around her neck. They decided they would always wear them for protection from whatever enemies Rupa warned them about. Something stirred deep inside them–something new and different. They tried not to think about the evil forces very often, because it made them both extremely nervous.

Summer faded into fall and school started in Bailey's Chase. On the first cool morning, the girls walked the three blocks to the century-old brick school, the school where all of Sparky's brothers and sisters had gone. The two cousins wore new clothes and colorful new sneakers. Each had a new book bag filled with school supplies. Sparky's book bag had pictures of superheroes all over it. Grey had chosen a plain silver bag, then stenciled scientific symbols all over it. Sparky had watched as Grey decorated the bag, but she couldn't quite understand why anyone would care so much about symbols of silver and gold and other elements. Grey told her it made the book bag look very academic. Sparky thought the superheroes were academic enough for her.

When they reached the school, Sparky led the way to the fifth grade classroom. She was anxious to introduce her cousin to the fifth-grade teacher, Miss Dooley.

"She's my cousin, but she's more like my sister–cause she lives with me," Sparky said exuberantly.

Grey stepped forward and said, "It's a pleasure to meet you, Miss Dooley," as she extended her hand.

Anyone could see that Miss Dooley, a rather plain shy woman, was pleased with Grey's good manners. "It's a pleasure to meet you, Grey," she said. "I hope you enjoy living in Bailey's Chase."

"She loves it so far, don't you, Grey?" Sparky interjected.

Miss Dooley laughed. "I bet she likes living with you, Sparky," she said. Although Miss Dooley had never taught Sparky in class, all the teachers knew her.

"Yes, I do," Grey replied. "Sparky keeps me laughing."

"We all need to laugh more," Miss Dooley said. Sparky hoped that attitude carried over into her classroom. Sometimes teachers said things like that, she thought, then expected you to be all quiet and serious all the time. She found it very confusing.

Miss Dooley took attendance and welcomed the new class. She found just the right seat for each student. She placed the boys who had reputations for fighting on opposite sides of the room. Peter, who wore thick glasses, took a seat near the chalkboard, and the tallest children were assigned to the very back seats. Miss Dooley gave Grey a position of great honor, a seat near the door, proclaiming that Grey would be her message bearer and errand runner for the first month of school. Everyone loved that position, because when you least expected it, you would be handed a note and sent on an errand in the building. It was great fun, walking the halls when no one else was there, while carrying a note of great importance to the nurse or principal or even to another teacher. Every month she would choose someone new for this honor, she told her class of wiggling fifth graders.

Grey took her job very seriously, going straight to the assigned destination and returning promptly to her classroom and then slipping silently into her seat by the door. On the other hand, Sparky would have probably taken the most scenic route, lingered as long as possible along the way, and possibly have even taken a peek at the note. Miss Dooley made a good choice.

Sparky took the same seat she'd had since first grade: front and center. She knew the teachers talked about such things on the playground, or when they ate their lunches from brown paper bags in the teachers' lounge. It was common knowledge among them that Sparky worked better when seated front and center. Otherwise, she would often get too involved in her neighbor's concerns and not stay on task. Although Sparky would have loved to see what school seemed like from other perspectives, she accepted her seat without a complaint. Sometimes she liked being in the front, like when the class got to watch a movie, or when Miss Dooley read books aloud and turned the book around so the students could see the illustrations. She loved it when her teachers read books to the class. Sparky always looked on the bright side of things. Her teachers liked that quality about her.

One crisp fall morning, several weeks later, Miss Dooley announced an upcoming contest. "Boys and girls," she said, "you know we have been learning about our Hoosier poet, James Whitcomb Riley."

The children nodded in agreement. They enjoyed it when Miss Dooley read his poems to them. Sparky wondered if kids all over the world listened to poems written by James Whitcomb Riley, or just in Indiana schools. Grey thought maybe children in other places wouldn't enjoy the slow, back-woodsy voice in the poems, but she found the Indiana pioneer dialect quite interesting.

"I'm very excited," Miss Dooley went on, "to announce a poetry contest for our class." Her eyes shone with excitement. "It won't be graded, so participation is not required. However, I encourage each of you to consider taking part. It will be such fun to memorize one of Mr. Riley's poems and present it on the stage in the auditorium." She waved her finger in the air and added, "There will be judges and a nice prize."

The class wiggled in excitement.

"You can just recite it or you can dramatize it," she said. "Some of you may want to wear a costume to show how that person might have dressed. Or, if you choose a longer piece, such as 'The Bear Story' you may read it. Whichever route you choose, I hope you will put your heart into it and make Mr. Riley proud of you. You will be judged on tone, clarity, and creativity."

The class was excited about the contest. Mr. Riley's poems had a way of making people feel like they were right back there in time, working on the farm, or going fishing. The teacher had made copies of many of the poems. After the last recess that day, she scattered them about on a table in the back of the room, so the children could each select one. She also displayed several books of his complete works along the chalk tray. The children spent the rest of the afternoon reading and deciding which poems they wanted for the contest.

That evening the girls made plans in their room. "I love the poem about the Raggedy Man. I love the way he waters the horses and feeds them hay and drives out the little old wobbly calf. I could pretend to be doing that as I talk," Sparky said. "I will dress like a hobo and recite it from memory. It's really not very long." Sparky usually made quick decisions in school matters.

Grey didn't answer. She lay on her bed, deep in thought, looking through the pages of the book of Riley poems she had borrowed from her teacher.

"What do you think, Grey?"

"Oh, excuse me Sparky," Grey said quickly. "Of course, 'The Raggedy Man,' that would be just right for you."

Sparky moved over to Grey's bed and sprawled out beside her. "Which one are you going to choose?"

"I think it will have to be 'Little Orphant Annie'. It seems appropriate for me, don't you think?"

The girls' eyes met solemnly. They had never discussed the fact that Grey was an orphan, although they both thought about it quite a bit. Ten-year-olds aren't very good at talking about death.

"I think it's probably the best one of all his poems," Sparky said. "And I think you would do a bloody-good job with it." She would have supported Grey with any poem she chose, but especially this one. Sometimes she saw Grey looking at the portrait of herself with her parents that sat on top of her chest of drawers, but neither Grey nor Sparky mentioned it. To Sparky, Grey was very brave and she admired her for it.

"Thank you, Sparky, I intend to. I will make all the orphans in the world proud of me."

Sparky marveled at how Grey always seemed to see things in a much larger scope than she did. "I have another idea," Sparky said. "The Raggedy Man picks apples in my poem. I'll put apples in my pockets, and when I come to that part I'll take them out and juggle them."

"You can juggle?"

"Well, I'm learning. I practiced with oranges a lot before you came. So far, I can only juggle two, but if I start practicing again, maybe I can do it."

Grey thought about it. "Apples, oranges, I guess it doesn't make any difference. I think the kids would love to see you juggle, and it would definitely impress the judges."

She continued. "I think I will do a dramatic presentation of my poem. I will dress like Little Orphant Annie and pretend to be baking bread, sweeping the hearth, you know, doing all the chores that she did."

"Bloody."

"And when I get to the part where it says, 'An' the Gobble-uns'll git you, Ef you Don't Watch out!' I'll face the audience, extend my arms, and be very scary." At that point, Grey stood on the bed and demonstrated her plan of action.

"Wow, you're good," Sparky said in awe. "I can hardly wait."

"*Hmmm,* I think my part needs some musical accompaniment," Grey said thoughtfully. "Yes, that would definitely make it better." She turned and faced Sparky. "Do you play anything?"

"No, but there's a piano near the stage and Miss

Dooley can play it."

"That's not exactly what I had in mind."

"I know! Newt plays a synthesizer–and he's really good at it!"

"What can he play?"

"Anything you want–he's very talented. Right now he's working on 'The William Tell Overture'. That is, when he's not messing with bugs."

Grey clapped her hands in delight. "Yes, that's perfect! Something classical to contrast with the country flavor. Let's go find him; I want to hear him play it."

For the next two weeks the girls practiced their presentations in front of the family, until everyone in the household nearly had the lines memorized too. Newt's music would add just the 'right touch' and his performance would be 'sterling' as he promised. Since he was in the sixth grade, they consulted his teacher, who agreed Newt could produce the music for Grey's presentation. In fact, they invited the entire sixth grade class to attend the grand event. Miss Dooley also invited the fourth graders, hoping it would inspire them to participate next year.

On the day of the contest, the girls woke early with excitement spilling from them like popcorn from a popcorn popper at the movies. After a hurried breakfast of oatmeal, (Sparky's mother always insisted they have something hot before school) they hustled off to school carrying shopping bags filled with their costumes and props.

The morning seemed to last forever, as it always does when something special is about to happen. Finally, lunch time arrived. Neither Grey nor Sparky had any appetite for the bologna and cheese sandwiches in their lunch bags. Instead, they nibbled nervously on chocolate chip cookies and sipped their milk through paper straws.

After lunch Miss Dooley sent everyone with costumes to the restrooms to change for the contest. When all seemed ready, the class filed to the auditorium where the judges–a retired teacher, Miss Rosella Poke, a banker, Mr. Cash Sweeney, and a member of the school board, Mr. Oswald Fife–sat at a table facing the stage. Miss Dooley had provided each of them with a bottle of water, a note pad, and a new pen. Leaning their heads together, the judges discussed how they would award points for each part of a performance.

The fourth and sixth graders filed into the auditorium and sat behind the fifth graders not involved in the contest. Sparky thought those kids must be really lazy, but Grey said they might just be too shy to perform. Those participating in the contest sat in the front seats. Grey sat on the end of the first row. Sparky sat right beside her.

Miss Dooley walked to the microphone in the center of the stage and cleared her throat. Then she tapped the microphone to make sure it worked properly. The audience, eager for the show to begin, became quiet.

"Welcome, boys and girls, to our James Whitcomb

Riley poetry contest. We have several fifth graders who have worked very hard to present poems for you. I'm sure you will sit quietly and give them your full attention." Her voice trilled with enthusiasm and expectations.

She introduced the judges and thanked them for coming. Then she walked back across the stage, high heels clicking on the wood floor, to the side, where she would announce each performance. Everyone knew Miss Dooley took great pride in her students.

The first poem told about goblins sitting on a fence, and was done by Sniffy and Snuffy, the Barnhouse twins. Their names were actually Stanley and Stephen, but no one ever used those names, since they were allergic to almost everything. Both boys had been sniffing and snuffing ever since kindergarten. Sparky found the presentation very boring, since they just took turns reciting the lines with little expression and used no props at all. After all, who could remember they were supposed to be goblins when they wore matching Spiderman T-shirts and jeans? If she were a judge, she'd definitely give them a low score, she decided. Maybe a 2 on a scale of 1 to 10. She squirmed and wanted to comment on it to Grey, but knew she was supposed to be quiet.

Next, Sarah Coleman marched up to the stage, dressed in a long dress with a shawl wrapped around her shoulders. She held a picnic basket on her arm and recited a poem about going out to 'Old Aunt Mary's' for dinner. Sparky hoped she'd never be called 'Old Aunt' anything. It seemed insulting to her. Both girls applauded politely for each contestant.

"Amaryllis Bailey," Miss Dooley called. Sparky snapped to attention. She jumped to her feet, checked to make sure the apples were still in her pockets, straightened the derby hat on her head, and proceeded to the stage.

The audience smiled at the little hobo on the stage with the patched clothes, the polka-dot tie, the funny hat, and the smudgy cheeks. As Sparky began her recitation, "Oh, the Raggedy Man, he works for Pa, and he's the goodest man ever you saw," the audience listened eagerly. When she got to the part about feeding the horses and driving out the calf, Sparky went through exaggerated motions for each activity. The judges watched her carefully, nodding to each other. Hers was easily the best performance of the event so far.

When Sparky came to the part about the apple picking, she reached into her pockets and retrieved the three apples. Her older brother had been teaching her to juggle three items and she'd gotten pretty good, if she concentrated and took her time. She had just begun when she looked toward Grey, in the front row, but found the seat empty. She scanned the audience for Grey's face, but Grey was nowhere to be seen. She couldn't imagine why Grey would leave the auditorium and miss her performance.

Troubled by the turn of events, Sparky lost her

concentration and the apples went flying all over the place. One rolled across the stage and onto the floor, one got caught in the curtains, and one popped Mr. Sweeney, the banker, directly on top of his shiny bald head.

The audience howled with laughter as Sparky did a mid-air dance trying to regain control of the apples. Miss Dooley attempted to quiet the children, but it was too late for that. When the children finally settled down Sparky apologized to the frazzled Mr. Sweeney, who was still rubbing his head. She tried to finish her recitation, but it had lost all of its previous charm.

Finally she returned to her seat amid the snickering children, disheartened. Sheesh, she thought, I probably got a lower score than those goofy Barnhouse twins. Mostly, she was curious about what had happened to Grey. She couldn't imagine why Grey would miss her presentation.

Miss Dooley's voice rang out, "Alexandria Greyling Bailey–next."

All eyes scanned the room, but Grey was nowhere to be seen.

Miss Dooley left the stage and came to where Sparky sat. "Grey must have gone to the restroom," she whispered. "Please go tell her to hurry; she's up next." At that Miss Dooley clicked back up to center stage and called for the next student.

Sparky shot up the aisle like a bullet. She hurried to the girls' restroom, and called Grey's name, but she didn't find her. Puzzled, Sparky started walking through the quiet halls of the school. The wing of the school that housed the older students was empty and quiet since the children and teachers were all in the auditorium.

"Grey," Sparky called as she walked up and down the corridors of the school. She peeked into the library and the nurse's office, but no sign of Grey. As she passed the janitor's room, she thought she heard a noise. She stopped by the door and called out her cousin's name again. "GREY!"

"Help me," came the faint answer.

Sparky pushed the door open and called again. Following her cousin's calls, she found herself against a closet door. "Grey! Are you in there?"

"Yes! The door is locked and I can't get out." Grey sounded desperate.

"What are you doing in there?" Sparky was baffled by the whole business.

"Someone gave me a note and said the principal wanted me to take it to the janitor. Then when I came into the janitor's room, someone turned off the lights, shoved me into this closet, and slammed the door." A sob escaped from Grey's distress.

"Who gave you the note?"

"Oh, I don't know–just a boy. He isn't in our class; he must be a sixth grader. Please, Sparky, get me out of here."

Sparky pushed and pulled on the door. She turned the

knob every which way, but it would not budge. "Hurry," Grey called, "or I'll miss my presentation."

"I can't get it; I think it needs a key. Should I try to find the janitor?" Sparky asked as she huffed and puffed from her efforts.

"Yes…No, wait, Sparky. I have an idea." Grey spoke softly.

"What?" Sparky was getting impatient with the whole matter. She didn't want Grey to miss her presentation, since she had worked so hard on it.

Grey spoke so softly that Sparky had to press her ear to the door.

"Let's try to use our…*power*."

Sparky snapped to attention. The girls had been careful not to use their power for fun since they had spoken with the Gypsy woman, Rupa. She had almost forgotten about the special gift they possessed, but this would be okay–this was an emergency.

"We have to both do it, Grey, at the same time," Sparky reminded her cousin.

"I remember," said Grey, calmer now and taking control of the situation. "Now, listen, Sparky. Put one hand on the door knob and the other on your magic charm."

"Okay, I got it," Sparky said as she reached inside her patched hobo outfit and fingered the earring hanging from her neck.

Grey continued with instructions. "Now, concentrate

on the door knob and think these words as hard as you can: *Open right now—open right now–open right now*!"

"I gotcha."

"Say it three times, Sparky, and start NOW!"

With one girl on each side of the door, both repeating the words and staring at the doorknob with all their might, the metal knob began to turn slowly in their hands. They heard a soft click from the lock.

"We did it," they both yelled.

Sparky immediately pulled on the door and it swung open. Amazed by the process, and still bewildered about this new power, the girls faced each other. Grey's eyes changed colors and sparks flew from Sparky's hair.

"Wow," Sparky whispered as Grey hugged her. "It worked. It really worked!"

"Let's hurry," Grey said as she grabbed Sparky by the hand. Together they ran from the janitor's room and down the hallway, to the school auditorium.

When the girls burst through the doors and into the auditorium, everyone turned and looked at them. Miss Dooley stood near the judges' table. She appeared very relieved. "Whew," she sighed, "You made it just in the nick of time. Hurry now, Grey, onto the stage."

The girls scurried down the aisle. Sparky dropped into her seat while Grey gathered up her things and advanced toward the stage. "Sorry, Miss Dooley," Grey whispered as she followed her teacher up the steps.

"And now, our last contestant of the day," Miss

Dooley announced to the anxious audience and the waiting judges. "Alexandria Greyling Bailey will be doing her dramatic presentation of 'Little Orphant Annie'."

Newt already sat in place by the time Grey reached center stage. She glanced at him and he nodded his head to let her know he was ready. As she recited the poem from memory, dramatizing every possible bit, the children stared spellbound. Newt seemed to know just when to play sections of 'The William Tell Overture' to accent the presentation.

When she completed her drama and took a low bow to the audience, the children and teachers stood, clapping and cheering loudly. Standing on her seat, until Miss Dooley noticed and motioned for her to get down, Sparky cheered and even whistled through her teeth. Amid all the applause, Sparky glanced toward the judges and thought she saw Miss Rosella Poke wipe a tear from her eye in sheer appreciation.

It didn't take the judges long to declare Grey the grand winner of the James Whitcomb Riley poetry contest. Grey bowed several more times, being very gracious in her response to so much attention and praise.

Miss Dooley commented on the students' wonderful presentations, then presented the gift-wrapped prize to Grey. After thanking the judges and audience, Grey opened the colorfully wrapped package.

"*Jane Eyre* and *Wuthering Heights,*" she said in

delight. "Oh, thank you Miss Dooley. How did you know that the Bronte sisters are my literary idols?" She clutched the prize to her chest. "I will treasure these books forever." Then Grey held up the boxed set of books for the crowd to see.

Sparky wondered if Miss Dooley had another prize ready in case someone won who didn't prize classical literature like Grey. She couldn't imagine Sniffy and Snuffy reading those books, or even pretending to like them. But then, she thought, maybe Miss Dooley knew all along that Grey would win the contest.

What Sparky didn't realize was Miss Dooley had several prizes ready: books about building model cars and kites, books about making jewelry, books about dogs and horses, and even a book of magic tricks, which Sparky would have loved. Miss Dooley always came prepared.

As they walked home that afternoon, carrying the bags filled with costumes and props, Grey asked, "By the way, how did your 'Raggedy Man' presentation go?"

"Bad. Be glad you missed it."

"I bet it wasn't that bad."

"Trust me on this one. It was awful." As an afterthought, she asked, "Why didn't you tell Miss Dooley about the note and being locked in the janitor's closet?"

"I thought about it, but then I didn't, because then I would have had to explain how I got out," Grey said simply.

"Oh, yeah," Sparky said. "That's right. We can't tell

anyone."

"You know that's going to be the hardest part of all this, not being able to share."

Sparky nodded.

The girls walked home keeping the fears, the dangers, and the secrets locked in their hearts.

Chapter Six

One sunny Saturday morning in late October, Sparky and Grey carried their bowls of breakfast cereal and glasses of orange juice outside to eat on the picnic table in the backyard. They always enjoyed breakfast on the picnic table; it gave them a chance to privately discuss their plans for the day. Sometimes they played in their tree house and spied on the neighborhood. It was a perfect place to read mysteries and pretend to be girl detectives, searching for clues and following leads. Since Saturdays always kept Mom busy in the beauty shop, it was a perfect time for the girls to be absent. Often they biked around town just looking for an adventure. Sometimes on Saturday afternoons, they went to the matinee at the movie theater on Main Street. No matter what they did, they always had fun together. Neither of them could imagine life now without the other.

When they reached the picnic table, they noticed an empty soda bottle sitting upright in the middle of the table. It hadn't been there yesterday. Upon closer examination they noticed a rolled-up piece of paper inside the bottle. They settled down on the benches on opposite sides of the table staring at the bottle as if it were an apparition.

"Why would someone stuff paper into a bottle?" Sparky asked as she slurped her cereal.

Grey's eyes lit up. "Maybe it's a message in a bottle."

"Like someone on a desert island might write and toss into the ocean?"

"Absolutely," Grey answered, eyeing the mysterious bottle with the paper inside.

"But we're not anywhere near an island or the ocean."

"I know, that's what makes it so interesting," Grey said.

"I bet someone is playing a trick on us," Sparky said with a grin. She shook the bottle several times, but the paper refused to come out. Finally she found a stick, turned the bottle on its side, and poked around until the paper slid out onto the picnic table.

Grey straightened out the paper and held it flat. Both girls read the words written in pencil on lined notebook paper.

Meet me on the swinging bridge at the scout camp. Be there at ten o'clock. Bring no one. Tell no one.

The girls' eyes met after they'd read the cryptic message.

"Bloody," Sparky said, still grinning. "It's probably Newt."

"Maybe not–maybe someone knows about our power," Grey whispered.

"How could they? We haven't told anyone."

"Maybe someone has been spying on us," Grey said in a mysterious tone.

The girls instantly looked around the back yard, but only saw the swing set they'd outgrown, a grape arbor, some flowerbeds, and a picket fence that separated the yard from the alley, from the street, and from the house next door where an elderly couple, the Snippets, lived.

"Who do you suppose it is?" Sparky asked.

Grey's face took on a determined look as she answered, "There's only one way to find out. Let's go to the swinging bridge at the camp."

"But the Girl Scout camp is always locked when summer's over," Sparky said.

"Surely there's some way we could get in. Is there a fence around the camp?"

"Yes, but maybe we could climb over it."

At nine-thirty the girls hopped on their bikes and headed for the Girl Scout camp at the edge of town. When they reached the main entrance, they found the gates chain-locked, as they had expected.

Sparky rattled the gates, shaking the chain and padlock. She looked up at the fence. "Do you think we could climb it?"

After looking up to the top of the eight-foot chain link fence, Grey said, "It would be really hard to climb chain link, and we'd probably snag our clothes if not our skin on those sharp barbs on the top. Surely there's a better way."

"Let's walk around it," Sparky suggested. "Maybe there's a place where we can crawl under, or a hole we can get through." In a few minutes, the girls had hidden their bikes in some shrubbery and were following the fence around the fifty-acre wooded camp.

As they had hoped, near a storage barn, they found a place where the fence had come loose from the post. It wasn't a big space, but just big enough for the girls to slip through. They soon found themselves standing inside the deserted camp.

"I feel like Peter Rabbit slipping into Mr. McGregor's garden," Sparky said with a giggle.

"Well, I hope you don't lose your jacket and a shoe like he did!"

"I promise to be careful."

Once inside, it seemed strangely quiet to the girls, because during every previous visit the camp had been hustling and bustling with pre-teen girls laughing and shouting and running every which way. Grey had only been there once, but Sparky had attended day camp every summer since turning seven years old.

Following a gravel road, they came to the shelter house. As expected, it was locked, the windows dark. The girls noticed the sky darkening. Thick clouds covered the sun and a chilly wind began blowing their hair into their faces. The flag that always waved over the camp had been taken down and cords slapped against the metal flagpole in the breeze, making a lonesome sound.

"Which way to the swinging bridge?" Grey whispered. She didn't know what made her whisper, but it just seemed like the right thing to do when trespassing.

"I'll show you," Sparky said, leading the way. As Grey followed they passed campsites, empty and silent, with picnic tables and fire rings for campfires. Some campsites still had clotheslines strung from tree to tree, where the girls had hung things that needed drying like dishtowels and wet socks.

They climbed a rather large hill and followed a leaf-covered trail into a thick wooded area. Dry leaves rustled under their feet as they walked between the trees. Leaves, swept off the trees by gusts of wind, fell like rain on the girls. After going down the hill on the other side, they finally came to the creek. It was about twenty feet wide and scattered with large rocks.

Although it was against the camp rules, Sparky loved to cross the creek by stepping on the teetering, slippery rocks. Only once did she slip and had to go home for dry clothes. The camp leaders had not been very understanding about the whole affair, and when she returned she found that the scavenger hunt had begun without her. While her campmates scavenged, she had been kept busy peeling carrots for the camp stew, which differed only slightly every day but always eaten by the hungry campers anyway.

"Now where's the swinging bridge?" Grey asked,

pushing strands of hair from her eyes.

"Down that way," Sparky said, pointing down the creek.

A narrow, rough path ran alongside the creek. It made walking difficult for the girls. In some places they had to climb over rocks and fallen trees. The creek rushed fast and high along its banks due to recent rains.

When they passed a small island in the middle of the stream, Grey paused. "Those two trees growing in the middle of that clump of dirt look like rabbit ears."

Sparky laughed. "You're right! I'd never noticed that before."

"Then from now on, let's call it Rabbit Island."

"Bloody good idea," Sparky answered. She had noticed that Grey liked to name things. Sparky figured that was because she always said she planned to write books someday, and people who write books have to name everything and everyone. She decided Grey would be good at that.

"How quaint," Grey said when she spotted the wooden swinging bridge that crossed the stream. "It looks like someone constructed it with ropes and giant Popsicle sticks." Grey had never walked on a suspension bridge and the prospect excited her.

Sparky had never thought about the bridge being quaint, but nodded. She agreed that it was an awesome bridge, but told Grey it was sometimes hard to walk on because it bounced as you crossed it. "You have to really hang onto the ropes," she said. "When you cross over, you're not in the camp anymore. That's private property over there, somebody's field."

"There's no one there," Grey said in a disappointed voice when they approached the bridge.

"Maybe we're a little early," Sparky said, checking her watch. "It's not quite ten yet, and the note said ten."

"Surely someone will come, after going to all the trouble of leaving us a note in a bottle," Grey reasoned. The girls scanned the area for the mysterious person.

"I still bet it's Newt just playing a trick on us," Sparky said.

Suddenly the girls noticed something that made the hair prickle on the backs of their necks. On the trail in the exact spot where the bridge began, someone had moved all the dry leaves aside and scratched a large picture in the dirt. It depicted a hand–a large, evil looking hand, like the hand of a witch with long twisted fingers and pointy fingernails. It reminded Sparky of the scary feeling she had when she rode the carousel with Grey on the night of her arrival, and it sent a chill up her back. In a moment of strange silence the girls looked at each other.

They immediately sensed danger. Each knew exactly what the other was thinking. Abruptly, the girls changed their minds. They didn't want to be at the isolated camp; they wanted to cross the bridge that would take them out of the camp and into a field. They knew they could run from there back to their waiting bikes.

All of a sudden the wind picked up even more and moved through the woods like an advancing army. Sheets of rain drenched them as they tried to decide which way to go. Whoever invited them here had not shown up, and the picture of the evil hand in the lonely woods made them afraid. They could almost see the Gypsy woman's face warning them of evil enemies.

"Let's get out of here," Sparky said.

"I don't want to go back through the camp," Grey yelled. "Let's cross the bridge."

Very slowly, hearts pounding, they stepped onto the rickety bridge.

Soon the girls were holding onto the ropes and treading very carefully over the wooden slats that made up the swinging bridge. It was tricky walking, since each step they took made the bridge lurch like a young colt.

Lightning flashed and thunder crashed through the camp. The girls stopped and clung to each other in fear. The wind caused the bridge to swing and tore at their hair and clothes, invisible hands reaching out for them. Unfortunately, the bridge was not in very good shape, and as Sparky tried to hurry along, her foot broke through one of the slats and she lost her balance. One leg went all the way through the bridge as she fell forward. Clinging to the rope, she called, "Help me, Grey!"

"I've got you," Grey said, pulling on Sparky's arm. With her help, Sparky got back on her feet.

"Wow! That was scary."

"Are you okay?"

"Yeah, I think so," Sparky said, but her leg hurt where it had been scraped as she fell.

With Sparky holding on tightly, the girls worked their way slowly across the shaky bridge, soaked to the skin by the pounding rain. Streaks of lightning lit up the sky and thunder continued to pound around them. An extra loud clap froze the girls in their steps when lightning struck a nearby tree and a banner of flames ran through it, before the rain extinguished it. The girls screamed in terror from the exploding noise and flash of fire.

"Keep moving," Grey urged. "We have to get across."

Sparky nodded and summoned up all the courage she could muster, wishing she had just stayed home. The girls continued to inch their way across the bridge, through the wind and rain, with Sparky limping behind Grey. The rain pelted their faces until they could hardly see, but they clung to the ropes and moved steadily taking tiny steps, the bridge swinging and bouncing under their feet. It was almost as if it had come to life just to work against them, making each advancing step a challenge to the wet, frightened girls.

Grey stopped abruptly and Sparky bumped into her. "Why did you stop? Let's get across," Sparky yelled over the wind and rain. Grey stood frozen in fear over the rushing stream.

Sparky peeked around her and saw a big boy with a dog at the other end of the bridge waiting for them. "It's *him,*" Grey said. "The boy who gave me the note at school."

"The boy who locked you in the closet," Sparky added, feeling suddenly angry and wanting to give the boy a good punch in the nose.

"Who is he?" Grey asked shakily.

Sparky stared at the boy with the shaved head and gold earring. His freckled face twisted with a sneering expression.

"I don't know him," she answered with a scowl. "But he's a sixth grader and he's mean. He's in trouble all the time. The kids call him Rip."

A large mangy-looking dog at the boy's side lunged and pulled on his leash, growling at the girls. They took a step backward.

The boy grinned at them in an evil way. "Sic'em," he yelled, releasing the snarling dog.

The girls stumbled backward in panic as the dog advanced, hair bristling along its back, teeth bared. Even with the high wind the girls could hear the snarls and growls of the vicious animal. Its eyes burned with rage as it lowered its thick body to the bridge and crept toward them. It seemed as if its whole purpose in life was to rip the two girls to shreds with its sharp teeth.

A horrible, sick feeling consumed the girls as they watched the dog move slowly toward them. However, it had trouble navigating the shaky bridge, and that gave the girls a few seconds to think. The mean-spirited boy advanced right behind his dog, holding onto the ropes on each side of the swinging bridge.

"Touch your charm," Grey yelled to Sparky as the terrified girls moved backward while clinging to each other. Sparky reached inside her sweatshirt and grabbed her charm. Supporting each other, they managed to reach the end of the bridge at the same time as the dog and boy reached the middle. The girls turned, pointed at their enemies, and called out in distress, "Bridge fall–bridge fall–bridge fall!"

With a deafening crack of thunder, lightning flashed again and the bridge split violently into two sections. The vicious dog and his sneering master tumbled headfirst into the swift moving waters below them.

The girls stood on the bank clinging to each other. They waited until they saw the pair surface and work their way to the other side. When Rip crawled up on the bank, cold and wet, he turned and glared at the girls with a look of pure hatred in his eyes. He raised his fist into the air and yelled, "Next time!" Then he and his dog, shaking, tail tucked between its legs, turned, and slowly headed back the same way they had come.

Grey and Sparky turned and tore up the trail, back through the camp, through the fence, and to their waiting bicycles. Hearts pounding, they pedaled as fast as they could toward home. The sky started clearing and the storm passed on its way, as summer showers are inclined to do. By the time the two sopping wet and shaky girls reached home, the sun had broken through the clouds once more.

They raced up to their room and changed into dry clothes.

"I've never been so scared in my entire life," Grey said, while she gathered up their wet clothes.

"Me, neither," Sparky admitted, pulling on dry socks.

"Now tell me about this boy Rip," Grey said as she put their wet clothes into the dryer. Her eyes changed to a darker shade as she faced Sparky.

"I really don't know much about him, except that he's in Newt's class and he gets into trouble a lot. Sometimes I see him sitting on the bench outside the principal's office. I think the next time I see him sitting there, I'll run in and tell the principal to give him the old 'what for'."

Grey didn't understand this old expression, but Sparky did. Her mom and dad had told her lots of times that if she didn't straighten up, they'd give her the old 'what for'. She knew it had to be a terrible punishment and planned to never find out for herself. However, it seemed something Rip deserved.

"So you think he's the one who wrote the note?" Grey asked as she dried her hair with a towel.

"He surely is. No one else showed up at exactly the time and place the note said."

"Why would he want to lure us out there on the bridge and then sic his dog on us? What did we ever do to him? We don't even know him."

"I don't know," Sparky answered. "Maybe the same reason he locked you in the closet–just because he's a mean no-good boy." Sparks danced around her head as she spoke. "I'd like to give him the old 'what for' myself." She made her hand into a fist and punched at an imaginary target in the air.

"Forget that, he's too big for you to tackle, Sparky. Let's think. There has to be another reason for him to pick on us. Remember what Rupa said?"

"Yeah, something about enemies who would try to hurt us. That really freaks me out, Grey. Maybe he's our first enemy."

"He seems young to be so evil," Grey said thoughtfully. "Maybe someone else sent him and told him what to do."

"Yeah, like some mean old uncle or neighbor."

"And he knows we can't tell on him, because then we'd have to explain being at the camp."

"Right. Then we'd be in trouble for trespassing, wouldn't we?"

"Yes, and maybe blamed for destroying the bridge."

"Lightning did that."

"Right, lightning."

The girls lay on their beds in deep thought. They wished they could share their questions and fears with someone, but no one would understand. Besides, they weren't allowed to tell anyone about their power. Somehow they knew that it was a fragile gift, and if they violated the rules in even the smallest way, it would disappear from them forever. It weighed heavy and worrisome on the two young cousins, more than any ten-year-olds should have to deal with. Overwhelmed with the whole situation, they stared at the ceiling until they both fell into deep and troubled sleep.

The autumn breeze lifted the curtains on the open window allowing a leaf to float into the room. It slid silently across the floor and came to rest directly between the girls' beds. While the girls slept, the only eyes watching the mysterious leaf were the eyes of the old elephant in the circus poster on the wall.

Chapter Seven

Rainy Sunday afternoons last forever when you're ten years old. Huge droplets of rain splattered on the roof and streamed down the windows of the old Victorian house in Bailey's Chase. Rain sloshed down the drain spouts. Puddles formed in the yards and street drains gurgled like huge thirsty reptiles. It was the kind of afternoon when parents napped, full from the dinner of pot roast and rich dessert, and older kids stayed in their rooms or ventured out to visit friends.

On this particular dreary day, Grey and Sparky lay on their beds and read Nancy Drew mysteries for over an hour. After that, they played every game from the stack of board games on the shelf in their room. Sprawled on the soft circular rug in the middle of the bedroom, Sparky won the games of Clue and Sorry, while Grey won Scrabble and Boggle. Sparky decided that Grey knew more words than the dictionary. Monopoly ended in a tie, as the girls lost interest in money and land titles. Neither girl really wanted to be a land baron nor cause the other girl to fall into bankruptcy, thus ending the game. They carefully stacked the boxes of games back on the bottom shelf of the bookcase in their room.

For a while, they drew pictures on the sketchpad that Grey had brought with her. Sparky listened, intrigued as Grey told her of the art classes she'd taken in her former life, as she liked to call the years before she came to live in Bailey's Chase. Sparky's eyes widened in interest and appreciation as she watched Grey's hands work deftly with sticks of charcoal and soft erasers. She was duly impressed as Grey sketched three-dimensional objects and then drew caricatures of all the family members. Finally, the girls bored of the art business too, and Grey put the sketchpad into her desk drawer.

"Hey," Sparky said suddenly, "I know what we can do."

"What?"

"We can go exploring in the attic. There's all kinds of neat junk up there."

"Your mother wouldn't care?"

"Naw, some of the stuff has been there for ages. We found lots of stuff up there when we moved into this house. It just came with the house. Of course, I wasn't born yet, but that's what the older kids told me."

"Who did the stuff belong to?"

"I don't know. I guess nobody does. Just whoever lived here a long time ago and left it all behind. Maybe it's the junk of several families, who knows?"

"Why would anyone leave possessions behind when they move?" Grey asked as she checked herself in the mirror and ran a comb through her hair.

"Mom says it's just junk and they didn't want to go to the trouble of moving it. I guess in the old days people didn't have garage sales or yard sales. They just kept their stuff and put it in the attic."

"Wow, we might find some treasures, Sparky." Grey's imagination immediately filled with ancient Chinese vases, Stradivarius violins, and ornate frames holding priceless art works, which had been painted over by amateurs.

"It's probably all worthless, but let's check it out," Sparky said. She slid the clothes to one side and opened the door on the back of the closet wall. She led the way up the narrow stairway. Grey followed closely at her heels.

In the darkness at the top of the stairs, they stumbled a little on the last step. Sparky said, "There's a string here somewhere that turns on the light." The girls raised their hands into the air and waved them about until Grey touched the thin string.

"I found it," she said. She pulled it, causing the light bulb to cast a dim light on the large musty room. It took a few minutes for their eyes to adjust to the dimness.

"Oh, this is *so* interesting," Grey said as she clasped her hands over her heart. "Why didn't we do this before now? I love this kind of adventure."

"I didn't think you'd think be so impressed. It's just a big old room that smells dusty with lots of boxes and furniture stacked around."

Sparky pushed an old rocking horse out of the way,

so they could move more easily into the main area of the attic.

"Well, I think it's positively charming," Grey said, as she looked around the big room. "It reminds me of the room where the sisters in *Little Women* put on their plays."

"We could do that, if we had two more sisters–sisters that weren't college age and gone all the time."

"Weren't Meg, Jo, Beth, and Amy lucky to have each other," Grey said dreamily. "Just imagine: Four sisters all growing up together and acting out plays. What could be more wonderful than that?"

Sparky had never thought to admire the March family, the family who enjoyed oatmeal. She wrinkled her nose when she thought about the father, who went off to war, and how one of the sisters died a slow and tragic death. It wasn't her favorite family, but she didn't want Grey to be disappointed in her, so she nodded in agreement.

The attic was actually the third floor of the old house. A small, dust-covered window sat under the roof peak at each end of the large open area letting in additional light. Boxes and trunks sat stacked along the walls under the eaves. Old discarded furniture sat here and there, some covered with sheets, adding a spooky atmosphere to the scene.

Grey giggled with delight as she twirled around, taking in everything. "I want to check everything out. I just don't know where to start." Sparky was pleased that she had something new to share with her cousin.

Soon the girls were lifting sheets and imagining the families who had sat in the creaky rocking chairs or written letters at the scarred desks.

"This baby bed is ours," Sparky said proudly. "We all slept in it. Mom says she'll bring it back downstairs when she gets her first grandchild. Wow! Just think, someday I'll be an aunt. That'll be so cool." When she noticed Grey didn't seem very excited about it, she added, "And you too! We'll both be the baby's aunts." That made Grey feel better and she smiled.

"What about this?" Grey asked as she examined an old dressmaker's model on a stand.

"Someone used it to make dresses, I guess," Sparky said as she patted the tummy area. "Someone kinda fat." Both girls giggled. They covered the model with a sheet. After a moment they decided it looked too much like a ghost like that, so they left it uncovered.

Shoving a stack of folded lace curtains aside, the girls opened a large trunk filled with clothes. The trunk lid squeaked as they propped it against the wall.

"Who do you suppose wore these clothes?" Grey asked as she lifted satiny dresses and scratchy men's suits.

"I guess people who lived here a long time ago. Dead people now."

Grey shuddered at the thought of dead people's clothes, but wondered what the people had been like. She pondered silently about their lives, if they had been boring or exciting. Had any of them done anything exotic like go on a safari through Africa or dance on stage with the Rockettes? She planned to take her clothes on a lot of exciting adventures when she became an adult. Plus, she'd leave a journal with her old clothes, so people who found them would know where the clothes had been.

Sparky lifted a hat with a veil and placed it on her head. "Look at me! I'm a fine lady going to catch a train." Grey handed her a crocheted shawl with a fringe, and she draped it around her shoulders. Then Sparky slipped her feet into a pair of high-heeled red shoes and strutted around the attic.

Grey laughed. "I shall call you Madame Concertina."

"Will you join me for tea?" Madame Concertina asked, bowing deeply.

"Of course, my lady. Just let me make myself presentable first," Grey answered while she dug into the trunk and found suitable clothes for herself. Not only did she find a purple satin dress and a pair of sparkly shoes, but she also found a large picture hat with a feathered plume rising from the band. Lastly, she handed Sparky a string of colored beads for her jewelry and slipped a strand of rhinestones around her own neck.

Soon the girls were costumed and acting out their little game of make believe. Satin swished as they walked around the attic. High heels tapped against the wooden floor. The closed trunk became their table, and pieces of mismatched cracked pottery became their fine china. It seemed to Sparky that Grey knew exactly what fine ladies would say at a formal tea and tried to keep up her end of the conversation.

When they tired of their dress-up clothes and tea party, they investigated a box of old books. They browsed through ancient schoolbooks with pictures of children in old-fashioned clothes. The buses and cars they drove looked even funnier than their clothes. A rather battered copy of *The Tale of Peter Rabbit* caught their attention, and they marveled how the illustrations looked the same as in the modern book. "I think it's lovely," Grey said, "that the illustrations are the same as they are today. That's what made it such a wonderful book."

They found biographies of George Washington Carver, Jane Adams, Clara Barton, Charles Dickens, and Mark Twain. Some of the books had leather covers and titles embossed in shiny gold letters. Sparky knew about some of the famous people, but Grey knew them all. The passing of time had caused most of the pages to become yellow and brittle. On some, the bindings had become loose, allowing pages to slip out. They glanced through an ancient blue-covered book about the San Francisco earthquake. They found stacks of paperback western novels and even an old cookbook with an old-style stove on the cover. They laughed at the hairstyle of the woman lifting a pie from her oven. "Her hair's almost as big as the oven," Sparky said with a laugh.

After a while, even the treasures of old clothes and books no longer held their interest. They investigated an iron birdcage on a stand and felt sorry for the birds that had been held captive there. They sorted through boxes of old dishes, most of which were chipped or cracked. An antique wicker baby carriage caught their interest and they considered taking it downstairs and cleaning it up. When they rolled the baby carriage away from the wall, they spotted an ornate oval mirror leaned against the wall.

"Gee, look at this old mirror," Sparky said. "I've never seen it before." She fingered the carved wood base and brushed dust from the crevices. It wasn't a large mirror. Most likely, it was designed to be placed on the top of a bureau.

"It's so old that the glass is all wavy," Grey observed.

"Hey, look at me," Sparky said as she bobbed up and down in front of the mirror, "I've got four eyes."

"Here, let me wipe the dust off so we can see better," Grey said. Sparky watched while she wiped a rag back and forth across the antique mirror.

Together the girls stared into the aged mirror filled with pockmarks and flaws. At first it seemed like an ordinary mirror, only distorting their reflections due to its age and condition, but then something happened. Something very bewildering and extraordinary. When the cousins leaned their heads together, cheeks touching, holding onto the sides of the ancient mirror, their reflections ceased to exist. Instead, a scene appeared,

slowly unfolding before them.

"What the bloody heck is that?" Sparky gasped, while sparks bounced around her head like miniature fireworks.

"*Shhh*…just watch," Grey whispered. "This is really weird."

Staring into the flawed mirror, they saw a foggy street scene. It was hard to tell exactly what it was with the fog and the flaws, but they could see buildings and streets. As they stared, spellbound, the scene slowly became clearer to them. They recognized their own town's courthouse and the steeple of the big downtown church.

"It's our town," Sparky said.

"It's like looking at a Christmas card scene of Bailey's Chase, but look–it's moving," Grey exclaimed, her eyes darkening with surprise and wonder.

"How can that be?" Sparky asked. Her gaze locked with Grey's and they both knew the answer.

"The magic again," they said in unison. A long moment passed between them before they bolstered up their courage and looked again.

When they pressed their faces close to the mirror, the scene slowly changed. It was as if someone had turned the focus knob on a camera and had cleared out the fog. It appeared as if that same someone had zoomed the scene in for a closer view. Suddenly they could see people walking on the streets and cars moving slowly through the downtown.

"It's Bailey's Chase–that's for sure, but some of the

buildings look different," Sparky said. She looked at Grey out of the corner of her eye. "I don't get it."

While they watched in breathtaking silence, the scene continued to change to the town park and then to the street where they lived. They recognized the neighborhood all right, but it looked wrong. The old band shell no longer stood in the park, and the playground equipment seemed new and different. Part of the school was the same, but it had a new addition on it. Some of the houses on their street were not the right color. The elderly Snippets' home next door was white, when it had always been gray, and the backyard held a swing set, like children lived there. Strangely, the pine tree that had just been planted in their front yard last fall stood suddenly tall and stately.

"This is weird. It's Bailey's Chase, but it's not Bailey's Chase," Sparky said.

"Sparky, look at the cars...they look so strange," Grey observed.

"Oh my gosh! I've never seen cars like that, except in science fiction comics."

"Look, there's someone walking down our street."

"Can you tell who it is?"

"No, it looks sort of like Newt's father, but it isn't."

"You're right; it looks more like Newt, but much older."

"Sparky," Grey commanded. "Don't look anymore." She suddenly pushed the mirror aside and pulled her cousin away.

"Why?" a bewildered Sparky asked, regaining her balance after being so abruptly yanked backward.

Grey's face took on a somber and scared look, eyes darkening with each word, "Because it's …it's the *future*– and we don't want to know that."

Sparky was puzzled. "Why not? I think it would be awesome to see the future."

"No, it wouldn't be awesome, Sparky, because it might hold something we don't want to see. Something terrible and tragic."

"I see," Sparky said, although she really didn't see at all.

The girls sat quietly for a few minutes, confused and stunned at the knowledge of what had happened. In whispered tones, Grey convinced Sparky that it was best not to know what the future held in store for them. She confided that she certainly wouldn't have wanted to know that she was destined to be an orphan.

"Yeah," Sparky said in agreement. "I guess you're right. If I knew I was going to be eaten by a lion or something, I'd rather not know. I'd just worry about it every day until it happened."

"Right," Grey said. "And you would probably avoid zoos and circuses for the rest of your life. Who knows? Maybe you'd even pass up a chance to go on a safari through Africa."

"That would stink."

"Right. Actually, Sparky, I really don't think it works that way. I think your destiny will pop up in your life and grab you whenever it decides to, and there's absolutely nothing you can do to change it. That's why they call it destiny. It just *has* to happen. You can't stop it."

Sparky nodded as if she understood, even though she didn't. However, she trusted this cousin who seemed to know everything from the mountain of books that she had read.

They carefully pushed the mirror back against the wall where they had found it and rolled the wicker baby carriage in front of it. After replacing items they had moved and leaving the attic as they'd found it, they turned off the light and went back down the narrow stairway.

Once back in their room the girls sat on their beds and stared at each other. For a while they didn't talk, but just tried to comprehend in their young minds what had happened to them. It gave them an eerie feeling to know that they had witnessed something so spectacular as a glimpse into the future.

They didn't understand their magical gift, but they respected it and kept its splendor locked silently inside themselves as they had been instructed to do. Touching the charms hanging around their necks offered some comfort to them. The charms would protect them from whatever enemies they might meet…after all, hadn't the Gypsy woman promised?

Chapter Eight

School continued and the days grew colder as fall turned into winter in Bailey's Chase. Leaves, once stunning with color, finally floated down to their final resting places to be raked, bagged, and set along the curbs for collection. Hooded winter coats replaced jackets. Furnaces chugged and whirred in their efforts to keep families warm. Fathers checked the anti-freeze in their cars. Mothers put blankets on beds and made huge pots of soup. Teachers set boxes of tissues on their desks for all the runny noses.

The girls worked hard at school each day and then hurried home to play outside for an hour or so before darkness claimed the day. Newt often joined them for a bike ride or a game of kick ball in the backyard, but some days he stayed inside and worked on his project for the school science fair. Sometimes Newt thought he had outgrown the girls with their talk of magic and make-believe.

Being a scientist, Newt demanded a scientific explanation for everything. Grey said that scientists weren't very creative, but Newt argued that scientists were extremely creative. After all, he reasoned, hadn't they invented *everything*? Then Grey and Newt got into a discussion on the right and left sides of the brain and how artists and writers are creative in a different kind of way.

Sparky listened, but she really didn't care much either way. She thought Grey and Newt were the two smartest people she'd ever known, and that was that. She interrupted their discussion with a question.

"Newt, what about the boy in your class everyone calls Rip?"

Newt straightened the glasses on his nose. "Ralph Smith. What about him?"

"Well, he's so big—how old is he?"

"*Hmmm.*" Newt thought for a moment. "I'd say he's probably supposed to be in eighth grade instead of sixth grade, so that would probably make him thirteen or fourteen."

"Why's he so bloody mean?" As usual, Sparky jumped right to the point on matters.

"I don't know. Why do you think he's so mean?" Newt always demanded evidence before he considered a matter or offered an opinion.

The girls glanced at each other. They knew they couldn't tell part of a story and not tell it all, and they knew they couldn't mention the magic that caused the bridge to spill Rip and his dog into the creek. Also, if they told about the locked door at school, they'd have to explain how they managed to unlock it.

Sparky continued, choosing her words carefully.

"Well, he lied to Grey about taking a note to the janitor once, and he sicced his dog on us." She frowned. "That makes him really mean."

Newt looked at Grey and she nodded in agreement.

Newt said, "I can't explain his motives, but one day Grey brought a note to our teacher and I heard Rip say, 'There's little Miss Goody-Two-Shoes from California'."

"Why would anyone not like Grey? She's nice to everyone," Sparky said.

"Maybe he's just jealous because none of the teachers would ever trust him to do anything," Newt said. "I don't know, but that's a theory."

"Why does he have to be so hateful?" Sparky said with a frown.

Newt sighed. "I don't know why he's so mean. My dad says his whole family is like that. They live in a shack down on the riverbank like a bunch of hillbillies."

"Do his parents just let him do whatever he wants?" Grey asked.

Newt shifted uncomfortably in his seat, because the first part of his next comment fit his own description as well as Grey's. "He doesn't have a mother. I'm not sure what happened to her." He paused for a moment, and then continued. "He lives with his dad, his grandfather, and some older brothers. My dad says they're just river rats and probably none of them has ever read a book in his entire life. All they do is fish, drink liquor, and cause trouble."

"Are they poor?" Sparky remembered that Rip's clothes had often seemed tattered and dirty. She always felt sorry for neglected kids who came from poor homes.

"They wouldn't be poor if anybody would work," Newt replied testily. "Dad says our taxes take care of people like them and he resents it. He says the system needs to change."

Neither Grey nor Sparky commented, because they didn't understand anything about 'the system' or taxes. However, if that's what caused Rip to be so mean, then they thought it needed to be changed.

One Saturday afternoon, the girls biked downtown and watched a Tarzan movie. Even though it was an animated version, they enjoyed it immensely. Afterwards, they stopped at the ice cream shop on First Street and bought ice cream cones with the last of their allowance. They sat at a small table inside the shop and ate their ice cream, instead of at the outside tables where people sat during warm days. While they twirled their cones and licked the ice cream into sharp mountain peaks, they talked about the movie and marveled at the bravery of Tarzan. They didn't know that soon they would be called upon to act very bravely too.

When they left the ice cream shop, they zipped their coats and pulled up the hoods against the chilly wind. The ice cream had made them cold all the way through, so the day seemed even colder than it actually was.

They pulled their bikes out of the bike stand by the front of the shop, turned them around, and had just started down the sidewalk when they heard a scream—actually, a cry for help, and it came from the alley running through the middle of the block.

"What was that?" Grey asked, trying to determine the direction from which the scream had come.

"Someone's in trouble. Let's go!" With those words, Sparky turned her bike into the alleyway, with Grey following right behind her.

In the distance they saw a cluster of people at the other end of the alley. As the calls for help continued, the girls pedaled harder. With the movie fresh on their minds, they felt a strong urge to help anyone who needed them, especially someone being mistreated by others. They were driven by curiosity as well, and could never have just gone on their way without investigating further.

When they got closer to the group of people at the end of the dim alleyway, they saw several boys surrounding an old man. "Help! Someone help me," the old man called weakly.

The teenage boys all looked rough. They pushed and pulled the old man around, trying to take something from him, but he held on for dear life. Groceries lay scattered all over the alley.

"Leave me alone," the old man called out in a voice both fragile and scared. Finally the girls could see that he was holding onto his wallet, while the boys tried to wrestle it from his hands.

"Let it go, Pop," a boy yelled into the old man's face.

"No," the old man yelled back as he struggled not to fall.

Neither the old man nor the boys saw the girls approach the scene.

"Leave him alone," Sparky suddenly yelled as she rode her bike right into the biggest boy. He immediately lost his balance and fell over backwards with a mighty *"Ooomph."* Grey gathered up her courage and did the same thing to one of the other boys.

The boys and the old man looked at the girls in surprise. For a second, no one moved or said anything. Shock registered on the old man's face. Anger registered on the boys' faces as they picked themselves up from the concrete. The third boy still held on to the old man's wallet.

Grey knew she had to think fast. "We've called the police and they're on the way." She lied with the most menacing look she could muster under the circumstances.

Then, standing astride her bike, Sparky screamed, hoping to attract someone's attention. Her parents had always told her to scream as loud as she could if anyone ever tried to kidnap her, and she decided this was a good time to try it out.

All three boys looked startled for a moment, then the one holding onto the old man's wallet suddenly let go. The man quickly dropped it into his pants pocket and took a step backward.

All of a sudden, a door opened into the alleyway, a back door from one of the businesses on the block. Sparky's scream had worked.

A big woman with a stern face called loudly, "What's going on out here?"

At that, the boys exchanged glances, then turned and ran down the alley. The woman came out and helped the man pick up his groceries. "Did they hurt any of you?" she asked.

"No," Grey said, "but they're bullies and they tried to rob this man."

The stern-faced woman wrinkled her forehead in thought and then said, "I bet I know exactly who they are, those no-good rascals. They hang around this neighborhood all the time, just looking for trouble to get into. I think I'll call the police and have them picked up."

The old man straightened his clothes and then introduced himself as Felix Truebody. His hands trembled when he shook hands with the girls and thanked them for trying to help. They knew they hadn't helped much, but maybe had made enough noise to attract the shop owner. The woman took the man into the store, promising to call a cab to take him home.

"I can't believe we actually did that," Grey said softly as she picked up her bike. "They could have turned on us." When she spoke and actually considered the danger they had put themselves into, her eyes changed like a kaleidoscope of colors.

"I'm not afraid of those bullies," Sparky said with bravado. "It took all three of them to pick on one old man. I bet they're scared of boys their own age. I bet my big brothers could handle them. Yeah, I'm sure they could."

Grey watched as sparks flew from her cousin's hair. She agreed. Once more the girls mounted their bikes and headed toward home. They didn't mention it, but inside, each girl was proud that she had helped the old man– proud that they had stood up for someone being mistreated. They felt a bit like Tarzan when he tackled animals much bigger than he was. Truly, they had helped to take a bite out of crime, as the TV commercial said.

They had only traveled a few blocks, however, when all good thoughts disappeared from the girls' minds. Pedaling around a corner, they came to a screeching halt when suddenly all three boys unexpectedly and completely blocked their path. Their scowling faces told the girls they wanted revenge.

"Now we gotcha," the biggest boy said as he grabbed the handlebars of Sparky's bike before she hardly knew what was happening. Her face blanched in fear as she tried to steady herself.

Another boy did the same thing to Grey, grabbing her bike and yanking it hard. She struggled to keep from falling onto the concrete sidewalk. The third boy stood nearby with his arms crossed over his chest and a sneer on his face. "Not such hot shots now, are you?" he asked as he leaned toward the girls.

"Let's teach them a thing or two," the first boy said in an angry voice.

"Yeah, let's teach them to mind their own business," the second boy added.

As the big boys advanced, obviously intending to beat them up, the girls panicked. Despite being smaller and younger, they were not about to stand by and be hurt without a fight.

"Leave us alone," Sparky screamed as she landed a hard kick into one of the boy's shins.

Grey sprang away from her bike and yelled, "Run, Sparky, run!"

Sparky took off like a bullet. Together they ran as fast as they could down the deserted sidewalk with the big boys right behind them. The girls searched frantically for anyone, but it seemed as if the whole town was asleep, leaving no one in sight.

However, the girls were agile and quick and had a head start on their pursuers. Their feet pounded down the sidewalk and around a corner. Still, they saw no one to help them.

"This way," Grey called when they reached the place where an alley met the sidewalk. They turned quickly into the alley before the boys rounded the corner. Just into the alley, they noticed a door standing slightly open.

"In there," Sparky called when she spotted the door. Together the girls almost jumped through the doorway and into the dark building. Pulling the door shut behind them, they huddled against the inside wall. Each girl held her breath while her heart pounded in her chest.

When they heard the boys' footsteps clatter past the door, the girls relaxed a bit.

"Where are we?" Grey asked shakily.

"We're in the back of the old movie theater. It hasn't been used for years."

"What if the boys come back and come in here looking for us?"

"We'd better not go back out into that alley," Sparky decided. "Let's see if we can find the front door of this building and go out on Main Street. We'll be safe there. There're always people on Main Street. They wouldn't dare try to hurt us in front of people. Somebody would call 911."

"What about our bikes?"

"We'll call Mom; she'll come get us–and our bikes. We have a bike rack on the front of the van. We use it when we take the bikes on vacation with us."

The girls started moving quietly toward the front of the old theater. Slowly they moved up a dark hallway, feeling their way along the walls. The floor creaked under them, lending an eerie atmosphere to the old deserted building. Finally, they came to the end of a hallway and entered a large, dim open area. Just enough light let them see doors with stars and fancy decorations on them and names of people who had used them last.

"These must have been the dressing rooms for the visiting actors," Grey said with interest.

"Yeah," Sparky said. "My dad said famous people used to do stage shows here–back in the old days."

Sparky wanted to investigate the dressing rooms, but Grey insisted they'd better keep moving. The boys might still be looking for them.

Finally, they made their way into the area behind the stage. They passed stacks of cardboard scenery left leaning against a wall and old dusty furniture scattered about, some covered with sheets. They saw lots of junk and discarded props from long-ago theater days.

Opening a creaking door, Grey found the stage. "Oh, Sparky, come in here."

They entered the stage and although it was dim, they could see how beautiful the theater had been in its day. Golden ties still held back scarlet velvet curtains, now shabby with age. The girls walked onto the center of the stage and stood quietly admiring the designs of gilded angels and chariots on the ceiling of the theater.

"Bloody," Sparky said, gazing at the ornate interior.

Grey's heart filled with rapture. She stood in the center of the stage imagining what it must have been like to perform in such a beautiful place. Her eyes changed to every possible shade of blue as she took it all in. She twirled about with her arms lifted high and then did a deep bow to an imaginary audience. For a few seconds the two cousins traveled back in time, becoming part of a troupe of actors performing in the glory days of the old theater.

Enchanted by their surroundings, the girls forgot about the old man. They forgot about the boys chasing them. They were so immersed in the beauty and grandeur of the old theater that everything else disappeared from their minds, and that was a bad thing. A very bad thing.

The moment shattered when a loud voice-a teen-aged boy's voice called out, "There they are!"

Staring in the direction where the voice had come from, the girls saw two of the boys standing at the end of the long aisle at the front of the theater. They stood between them and the door to Main Street.

"It won't do you any good to run, cause we've got you now," one boy called. "And we left Spike guarding the alley door, so you won't get away this time."

"Yeah," said the other boy with a sneer. "Let's show them what happens to little girls who interfere with our plans. Let's give them a good pounding." Then he curled his hand into a fist and thumped it hard into the palm of his other hand.

Chills went up their spines as the boys started down the aisle toward the stage where the girls stood, frozen in fear, hearts racing.

In desperation and terror, the girls clung to each other. Eyes darting, they realized there was no way out. No way to get away from these hoodlums.

"Please, someone help us," Grey said, almost in a

whimper. She shot a terrified glance at the boys. *Trapped!*

"Please," Sparky added, shaking with fright and near tears.

Each girl reached for her charm, almost without thinking, while the boys slowly moved toward them. Although it was mean and cruel, the boys looked excited when they realized how much they had frightened the girls.

Strangely, without any warning, everything changed. The overhead lights popped on. Brilliant spotlights beamed onto the stage. Music roared from the loud speakers located on both sides of the stage and along the side walls. The empty, desolate theater had somehow awakened and come to spectacular life. They'd been thrust into the middle of a magnificent performance.

The girls watched the unfolding drama with wide unbelieving eyes.

"Wow," Sparky said. "This is fantastic."

"I can't believe it," Grey whispered in astonishment.

The boys stood with their mouths open in shock and surprise.

With a drum roll and a flash of light, the back curtains parted and a clown stepped into the bright spotlight. He wore a coat covered with large red polka dots, and a flower stuck into the lapel. Gold sparkles covered his vest that lapped over his knee-length pants. Striped stockings covered his lower legs and disappeared into huge funny shoes. Without a word he began turning handsprings across the stage. When he reached the middle of the stage where the girls stood spellbound by all they saw, he stopped, lifted his derby hat, and took a deep bow. Slowly he straightened to his full size and stood facing the girls in silence. Then, to everyone's total surprise, he brought his hands from behind his back and handed each girl a colorful bouquet of fresh flowers.

"Th-thank you very much," Grey said when she finally found her voice.

"Yeah, thanks," Sparky squeaked, still overwhelmed by the dazzling performance.

The clown smiled widely showing a gap between his two front teeth. Deep dimples appeared in both cheeks. After carefully replacing his derby hat over his red hair, he twirled his fingers in a good-bye wave and said, "Good night and God bless." Then he walked back into the curtains and vanished from sight.

After staring at each other in total surprise and shock, the girls suddenly remembered the boys. They cautiously glanced around for them, but the boys had disappeared. Being cowards, they had run away when the clown appeared.

"Let's get out of here," Sparky said. She knew that something strange and wonderful had happened, and didn't want to push their luck by hanging around in case the boys returned.

"Yes, let's hurry," Grey said. They quickly found their way to the front doors of the theater. Soon they stood safely on Main Street. People passed by, as on any ordinary day, going about their business. Nervously, Sparky and Grey scanned the sidewalk in both directions, but the boys were nowhere in sight. The girls looked back at the old theater, all dark and desolate, as it had been for many years. Not a bit of life or light or music—just an old theater, empty and silent as a tomb.

Cautiously, the girls walked down the sidewalk and around the corner. Hugging the wall, they peeked into the alley. No boys. They retraced their steps to where they had left their bikes and found them leaned neatly against the wall waiting for them. Hurriedly, they mounted their bikes and headed straight for home, fresh flowers tucked under their arms.

When they burst into the kitchen at home, Sparky's mom, whom Grey now also called Mom asked, "Well, did you like the movie—and *where* did you get those flowers?"

"Someone gave them to us," Sparky said truthfully, as the two raced through the kitchen and up the stairs.

Once safely in their room, they sat on their beds and tried to sort out what had happened.

"That was so unreal," Grey said shaking her head in disbelief. "Absolutely unreal. Rupa was right: Good and evil. We did something good by helping the old man, and immediately we were in danger from evil boys."

"I was so scared I think I almost wet my pants," Sparky confessed.

"Fantastic, that's what I'd call it," Grey said, still shaky from the incident. "You know," she said thoughtfully, "we really should keep a journal about all of this."

"No way," Sparky warned. "Someone might read it."

"I guess you're right. We can't take that chance."

Later, Sparky found a sand bucket, tripped down the hall to the bathroom, filled it with water, and placed the flowers in it. She settled it on the top of the dresser the girls shared. Carefully, she touched the flowers and noticed their fresh, dainty petals. She wondered where they had come from. They looked as if they had just been picked from a garden in some warm place, certainly not from anywhere in cold, wintry Bailey's Chase. Without a doubt, they *were* real, as real as anything in the room–not just figments of anyone's imagination.

After dinner that evening, Sparky lay on the couch watching a western movie while Grey booted up the computer. Silently, Grey searched for information about clowns. She read about clowns who performed with circuses, clowns who traveled with Vaudeville shows, even movie and television clowns.

When the rest of the family had left the room, Grey said urgently, "*Psst* Sparky, come here."

Sparky put down her bowl of popcorn and ambled over to the computer. She stared at the colorful picture on the monitor.

"It's *him*," she whispered, sparks dancing in her hair.

Grey smiled. "I'm sure it was him. He's a famous clown, Sparky."

"But why...how?" The picture left Sparky nearly speechless.

Grey scrolled down to the print under the clown's picture and continued to explain as her cousin stood, totally confused by the whole matter.

"He's been dead for quite a few years, but it says here that he grew up in this town." She turned to face Sparky. "I bet he performed on that very stage when the theater was all new and beautiful."

Sparky read the words over the picture. "His name is Red Skelton."

Chapter Nine

Grey missed her parents, but she enjoyed the holidays with her new family. For the first time she shared a turkey dinner with a whole table full of relatives. Christmas arrived in exciting new ways, with Sparky at her side. Together, they chose the right tree for Dad to chop and helped to haul it home. Mom furnished popcorn and cranberries and let the girls fashion garlands for the tree. One day they all baked cookies and delivered them to nursing homes. On Christmas morning, the girls found matching ice skates under the tree. That afternoon, they learned to skate on the pond at the city park. After many falls and bumps, the girls mastered the art of ice-skating, all on their own. Christmas had its own brand of magic and the girls reveled in it.

Before she moved to Bailey's Chase, Grey had never experienced snow. When it arrived she thoroughly delighted in the flakes, the softness, and the silence of it. For the first time, she learned about 'snow days' and cheered with Sparky as they watched the TV for news of school cancellations. Several winter days became unexpected vacation days. One day Newt helped them to make a snow family in the front yard complete with pets.

Another day the three coasted down snow-covered hills on the old family sled, laughing and tumbling into the snow at the end of each ride.

Although the girls certainly didn't forget about the magic, they didn't seem to need it during the cold winter months. Things had settled down in Bailey's Chase, so they kept the magic tucked away in a secret place. That was okay with them. They had fun just being together and being normal fifth graders.

Spring finally pushed winter aside and moved into town. Daylight lasted longer. Daffodils bloomed and lawns became green once more. The girls rode their bikes and played kickball with Newt after school. Just when Grey didn't think life could get any better, Sparky told her about the field trip that each class got to take in the spring. "It's usually the best day of the whole school year," Sparky told her. Grey excitedly awaited her first field trip at her new school.

"Remember, boys and girls," said Miss Dooley, as she faced her class. "Tomorrow is our field trip. We are going to visit some of the historic sites of our town. We are very lucky to live in such an historic place."

The class collectively wiggled with anticipation as she reminded them of their roles as good citizens. "We will wear our best manners tomorrow, since we will be representing our school." She shook her finger as she spoke. "Full attention and no talking while the guides are speaking. Remember to stay with your partner at all times and never leave the group." She looked over the whole class, but Sparky thought she looked at her just a little longer than anyone else. Okay, she admitted to herself. Maybe she had wandered off a little on previous field trips, but she'd grown up since then. Taking a deep breath, she glanced around to see if any of her classmates' eyes had zeroed in on her. She relaxed a bit when she realized the other kids were too excited about the trip to be thinking about her.

"Now, did everyone return his or her permission slip?" All heads nodded as the children grinned at partners already chosen. "Don't forget to bring a sack lunch and a can of soda for the cooler we will have on the bus." After a moment's pause, she added, "Oh yes, some of you may want to bring money to buy a souvenir."

That night the girls could hardly sleep for the excitement of the upcoming field trip. Any diversion from the regular school day promised fun and adventure. Little did they dream that their day of fun and adventure would far surpass that of the rest of the class.

When they packed their lunches the next morning, Mom reminded, "Be sure and put some nutritious foods in there. Remember you're growing girls."

"We are," promised Sparky, as she scooped up the two small boxes of raisins that her mother set on the kitchen counter. She tossed one to Grey, who tucked it into her lunch sack, which already held a sandwich, some carrot and celery sticks, a banana, and two Girl Scout cookies.

Before coming to Bailey's Chase, Grey had never packed a lunch. The housekeeper took care of those matters. She turned her mind quickly away from those days, as she always did when memories arose that could make her sad. It was impossible to be sad in the constant company of the bubbly Sparky, not to mention the unusual and exciting adventures she'd experienced since she'd arrived in this family and town. Some days she almost forgot she'd had a life without Sparky.

Mom gave them each two dollars to spend for a souvenir, and they tucked the money into the pockets of their jeans. After zipping their jackets and giving Mom the usual good-bye hug, they set off for school, each carefully carrying her lunch and can of soda.

As they walked the three blocks to school, Grey asked, "Do all the classes get to see these historic sites?" She still had plenty to learn about the ways of the school and community.

"All fifth graders, since they've already studied Indiana history," Sparky answered. "But by the time we reach fifth grade, most of us have already seen this stuff– or at least part of it. But I guess some kids haven't. And I've never been on the guided tours, just wandered around these places with my family."

"So..." Grey ventured thoughtfully, "what kind of field trips do the other classes get to take?" She decided it would be fun to look forward to the standard field trip for next year.

"It's like this," Sparky explained as if in charge of the whole business. "First graders always visit a farm. They think it's really cool to pet the baby animals and all."

"I'd like that," Grey said.

"Too late. Only first graders get to go." After glancing at her cousin's disappointed expression, she added, "Maybe Dad will take us sometime. He knows a guy who raises all kinds of animals–even llamas."

Grey nodded with a smile. Sparky continued. "Then you're in second grade and you get to ride a train. They think it's a big deal. The bus takes them to the train station over in the next town, and they walk to a park and have a picnic. Then they ride the train home." She thought for a moment and added, "It's actually pretty cool. The engineer gives everyone a paper railroad hat and a train whistle. You can wear the hat, but you have to leave the whistle in the package. I guess the adults would freak out if all those little kids started blowing their whistles at the same time. Anyway, it's always fun to ride the train." Grey didn't say anything, because she had ridden lots of trains.

Sparky went on. "Now, third graders all go the Shrine Circus in Evansville. I liked that, especially the trained animal acts. They had these neat bears that wore sunglasses and funny hats and could ride motorcycles. I just about laughed my head off. And they had great souvenirs–that's where I got the elephant poster in our room."

Grey nodded and a look passed between the girls, each remembering the day they had experimented with their power and caused the elephant in the poster to move. For them, everything changed on that day.

They walked in silence for a moment, then Grey asked, "Where do fourth graders go on their field trip?"

"The zoo in Evansville. It's fun. We picnicked right there in the zoo park. We rode a train that took us all around. Then we got to wander in small groups with a room mother."

"I love zoos," Grey said quietly, remembering trips to the San Diego Zoo and how she loved the koala bears there.

"Me too. I love the monkey house most of all."

Grey smiled. Somehow, that didn't surprise her at all.

"What about sixth graders?" Grey decided it would be fun to have next year's field trip to look forward to.

Sparky's eyes lit up in excitement. "Oh, it's the coolest trip of all. They get to ride a chartered bus, not a school bus, all the way to Indianapolis. It even has a bathroom on it, and it takes three hours to get there. The bus ride is so much fun, it's almost like a field trip all by itself."

"Where do they go when they get to the city?"

"The Children's Museum. I can hardly wait. It's filled with neat stuff about science. Newt will get to go this year. They always go on one of the last days of sixth grade, just before school is out for the summer."

"It sounds like a place Newt would love," Grey decided as they turned in to the sidewalk that led to the school.

"Yeah, Newt: Mr. Science. He'll probably run the place someday," Sparky said as she kicked a pebble off the sidewalk. The girls laughed at the idea of Newt being the director of the Children's Museum.

"He'd probably not even go home," Grey said with a giggle. "He'd probably bring a bed in and sleep right there among the exhibits."

"Wouldn't it be funny if a dinosaur came to life and chased him around, like in that movie?" Sparky said. They laughed at the thought.

After taking attendance, Miss Dooley and two room mothers led the class to the waiting school bus for the ride to the historic sites of the town. The field trip had begun.

The girls deposited their cans of soda into the cooler at the front of the bus, then settled onto a cool leather seat. Riding a bus was fun for them, since they walked to school each day. Sometimes they envied the country kids, who woke early and clambered onto the big yellow and black school buses that stopped at the end of their country lanes.

When the bus stopped, Miss Dooley stood near the driver and reminded the children of what they had already been told several times that week. "Our first visit will be to the George Rogers Clark Memorial, boys and girls. It's important to know that this is the biggest memorial in the country, outside of Washington D.C. I'm sure you remember how we studied about this brave soldier who won important victories in the Northwest Territory during the Revolutionary war. His victories gave our country its chief claim to land west of the Mississippi River and north to the Great Lakes in peaceful negotiations with England." The children listened, blinked, and nodded. "He captured the town in 1779 by forcing the British to surrender Fort Sackville, which controlled the town."

Like good soldiers the children followed Miss Dooley into the memorial where they viewed large murals depicting the historic events. They listened on headsets and relived that moment in time. As they filed out of the building they decided they all loved George Rogers Clark and vowed to themselves to be patriotic Americans forever.

"Now," Miss Dooley announced as her scarf blew in the wind, "notice the bridge. The Lincoln Memorial Bridge spans the Wabash River where Abraham Lincoln's family crossed when they moved from Indiana to Illinois in 1830."

Sparky squinted her eyes toward the bridge and could almost see the boy Abe Lincoln walking beside the wagon filled with his family's possessions, just like the picture in her social studies book. How exciting it would have been to know Abe Lincoln as a boy, she thought.

Miss Dooley's voice brought Sparky out of her daydream. "Now, children, gather around the statue of Francis Vigo for a group picture." Obediently the youngsters stood in front of the huge statue of the kind-looking man seated in a giant chair at the riverbank. Sparky couldn't remember what part he played in history and decided to ask Grey when they got home. Grey always remembered important things like that. Sometimes Sparky thought living with Grey was almost like having her own search engine.

After handing a camera to one of the room mothers, Miss Dooley stood in the midst of her class and smiled widely for the picture. It would be duplicated later and sent home with each child. It was something Miss Dooley always did for her classes.

Since the bus driver had conveniently parked the bus by a grove of trees near picnic tables, the children easily scampered onto the bus to retrieve their cans of soda and lunch sacks. They gathered around the tables for lunch. Despite the crispness of the April day, it was sunny and the children wore jackets, making it perfect for a picnic lunch. It would have been no fun at all to eat lunch on the bus, as they would have been required to do on a rainy day.

No one laughed about Sparky's peanut butter and tomato sandwich, since they had seen her eat them several times. However, they appeared interested when Grey explained how natural a corned beef and jelly sandwich was, almost like roast lamb and mint jelly. Since none of the children had eaten roast lamb and mint jelly, they kept their opinions to themselves.

Once everyone carefully dropped their lunch remains into a nearby trash can, the class climbed back onto the bus for the short ride to the next points of interest. They visited a small building, which at one time had been a newspaper office, back in the olden days. An adult volunteer, dressed in pioneer clothes, gave a short talk about the old-fashioned printing press. He held up a newspaper and explained to the class the similarity to the first one printed in the state. The class didn't find this very interesting and were beginning to yawn when Miss Dooley rounded them up and led them down a sidewalk to their final destination.

"Grouseland," she said triumphantly as she stood on the front porch of the beautiful old mansion. "This is where the legislature of the Indiana Territory held its first sessions. William Henry Harrison built it when he served as the territorial governor. He lived with his family in this house, and it has been restored to its original state," she went on. "We are going to break into small groups and some of you will go with the room mothers through this house. Be sure and notice the bullet hole in the shutter of the dining room window." The children snapped to attention as she spoke. "That is where a Native American shot a rifle at Governor Harrison while he carried a child across that room. Luckily, no one was hurt, and the hole made by the bullet was never patched, so it would always serve as a reminder of the dangers surrounding those who lived in this house."

Soon the kids headed off in different directions throughout the beautiful old home. The guides pointed out the antique dishes, furniture, and wall decorations. No one was disappointed in the bullet hole in the shutter.

Grey took a special interest in the schoolroom where the children of the house were tutored. She marveled at the old writing desks, books, and slates. Sparky liked the children's bedrooms best, with the old-fashioned beds and toys. Neither girl had much to say about the kitchen with its iron cookware and open fireplace. They couldn't imagine any tasty food being prepared in such a crude way. They listened carefully as the guide pointed to the round table in the parlor where Governor Harrison signed treaties with the Native Americans. Staring into the parlor, they could almost imagine those Native Americans in feathered headdresses and colorful costumes facing the ruling white men and nodding in agreement to their terms.

Although no one mentioned it, the girls knew the tiny, stuffy rooms under the eaves had been designed for the slaves who did the work in the house. When the group filed through the slave quarters, Sparky and Grey noticed a child, an African American child, standing in one of the corners staring at them with sad eyes. The little girl appeared to be about their age. She wore old-fashioned clothes. They weren't fancy colonial clothes like the volunteer ladies wore, but clothes like slave children wore. They stared silently at her braided hair, her faded cotton dress, and her bare feet.

No other school groups had toured the house, so they wondered where the child had come from. No one else seemed to notice the girl. Just as Sparky started to wave her hand and speak to the child, the child put her fingers to her lips in a well-known sign that meant, "*Shhhh.*" She said nothing, but watched them with sad eyes as they passed from the room with their group. The girls shrugged their shoulders and exchanged a puzzled look.

Before the tour ended the guide mentioned a secret tunnel through which the family could escape to the river if ever attacked.

"Where is that tunnel?" Sparky asked. It was exactly the kind of thing she loved.

The elderly guide in the colonial costume smiled. "Oh, we don't know. The records mention the tunnel, but it must have been sealed many years ago, because we've never found it."

"Now," the teacher announced, "you may have the last fifteen minutes to look around some more or to buy something from the souvenir stand in the basement. But be sure to be back on the bus at three o'clock, because we have to return to school on time."

Children scattered in several directions amid the smiling helpers. Most went to the souvenir stand, but a few wanted to return to their favorite part of the house for one last look.

Grey pulled Sparky into an alcove. "Come with me," she whispered. Then she turned and led the way down a back staircase. Sparky followed her through the large kitchen rooms and past the souvenir room. When she reached a closed door, she faced Sparky and spoke excitedly. "This is the only part of the house we haven't been shown, so I bet the entrance to the tunnel is in here."

"But," Sparky began, "the guide said no one knows where it is."

"That may be true, but just think, Sparky. If it leads to the river, it has to be on this side of the house."

Suddenly, Grey stopped talking and gestured to Sparky to turn around. As she did, she saw the strange girl again; this time she made her way slowly toward them. When she reached them, she spoke for the first time. "If you're looking for the tunnel, open that door and I'll show you where to find it."

Glancing both ways to make sure no one would see them, they lifted a bar from its place and slowly pushed the door open. Stepping aside silently, they allowed the girl to enter first. Once inside, they closed the heavy wooden door. Two small windows up high on the wall allowed enough light for them to see.

Puzzled by the strange barefoot child, they watched as she motioned to a section on the wall. "This is a new wall," she said. "The entrance to the tunnel is right there. They bricked over it a long time ago."

"Why?" Grey asked softly. "It would be interesting to see."

"It wasn't safe anymore. They feared it would cave in on someone."

"Why are your feet bare?" Sparky suddenly asked when she could no longer stand not to. "Aren't you cold?"

The girl smiled for the first time and shook her head no. Her black braids swung over her face.

"Why did you motion for us to be quiet back there?" Grey asked.

"Yeah," Sparky said, "we were just trying to be friendly."

The dark-skinned girl just smiled mysteriously at them.

Grey stared at the strange girl for a moment before speaking. Then she said slowly, "I think I know why, Sparky. It's because we are...the only ones who *can* see her."

Sparky gulped and stepped closer to her cousin.

The girl's sad eyes answered the question for both of them.

Grey whispered, "Who are you and why can we see you here? Please tell us."

The girl looked down and dragged her bare toes over the floor. Sparky and Grey waited. After a few seconds, she looked up and spoke. "My name is Calico, and I knew you could see me. Those other kids could never see me. I don't know why."

"Where do you live?" Sparky asked.

"I don't live nowhere," the girl said sadly. "I just hang around here. Been hanging around here for so many years I don't even know how many."

"Are you a...a g-ghost?" Sparky asked, hoping she wouldn't faint dead away and embarrass herself.

The girl tucked her chin down as if embarrassed. "I guess so. I just know I did live here a long time ago. My mama and papa worked in this here house for the rich folks. Governor Harrison was a good man. He freed his slaves, but lots of them, like my folks, didn't have nowhere to go, so they just stayed on and worked for him."

"Please tell us what happened," Grey said as if she dealt with this kind of situation every other day.

"My mama got sick and died from the pneumonia fever, the same fever that got my little twin brothers. They all went to Heaven, I guess. I wasn't very old." She paused in thought. "Then my papa got in trouble for something he didn't do, and the sheriff and his men hanged him."

"*Hanged him,*" Sparky said so loudly that Grey shoved her elbow into her side to quiet her. Sparks danced fiercely around Sparky's head, but if the girl noticed them she didn't say anything.

"They said he stole some horses that belonged to a white man, but he didn't. He was just a'movin' those horses for that man. He asked him to move 'em for the summer to a better pasture. I heard the man ask him to do it—said he'd give him a quarter."

"Did your dad tell the sheriff that?" Grey asked.

"Yeah, but they wouldn't listen to a slave's talk. The man who told him to move the horses went off on a cattle drive and got killed. He never came back, so he couldn't tell nobody about it."

The girls waited silently as they watched the girl, this ghost, this spirit, who stood before them. Finally, Sparky asked, "What happened to you?"

The child twisted one of her braids around her finger as she answered. "Oh, I went to live with some neighbors. It was okay, but I sure missed my own family."

"Then what happened?" Grey asked kindly.

"Well, it just seemed like everybody was getting sick of something or the other. The whole family I'd been staying with got sick with Scarlet Fever, but they all got well."

"And you?" Grey asked.

"Me? I just reckon I didn't have enough spirit to get well. I just got weaker and weaker until one day I finally...."

"*YOU DIED?*" Sparky almost yelled, but she couldn't help it. She had never talked to anyone before who had already died, and the whole scene creeped her out. She took deep breaths to try to calm herself down.

"I reckon I did. All I know is I just kinda floated up out of my body one day, and I been hanging around here ever since then."

"Why didn't you go up to Heaven to be with your family?" Sparky asked.

The girl paused for a moment and looked at her feet. When she looked back up, tears ran down her cheeks. She brushed them away with the back of her hand. "There's sumptin' I gotta do first–then I'll go."

"What?" the girls' voices rang in chorus.

"I just can't go until I clear my papa's name. When I go to Heaven to be with him and Mama and my brothers, I want to be able to tell them that people here know about Papa being a good man–not a horse thief."

"But it's been so long ago. How could you do that?" reasoned Grey.

"Yeah," added Sparky. "Everyone's dead now that lived back in those days."

"Papa got that quarter on my birthday. I just know the man wrote it down in his big store ledger book. If I could find that book, I could prove it."

"Where do you think that book is?" Grey asked quietly.

"I don't know, but I know his name and I know he ran a store. Sometimes families keep books like that."

"Maybe we could help you," Grey said. "Tell us everything you know."

"Well, his name was Russell Tanner and he ran a general store in town. I just know he wrote everything down in his big account books. That was mighty important to store keepers."

"Do you know when it happened?" Grey asked.

"I remember because Papa took me to the store and let me pick out a new doll for my birthday. I turned eight years old on June 3, 1810. My papa's name was Isaac. Isaac Washington."

"*Hmmm*," Grey said thoughtfully, "maybe the library would be a good place to start."

Calico's eyes brightened. "You really will try to help me prove my papa's innocence?"

"Sure we will," Sparky said confidently. "We have a friend named Newt, and he can figure out how to do everything. Maybe he'll help us."

Tears filled Calico's dark eyes again. "I will be forever grateful to you."

Suddenly the sound of a whistle filled the air, Miss Dooley's signal for everyone to board the bus and return to school.

"No promises," said Grey, "but we'll see what we can do." Sparky nodded in agreement.

"I'll be right here waiting for you," Calico said.

The girls waved good-bye and hurried to find their seats on the already crowded bus. It was too late to buy a souvenir, but they didn't care. They had a memory from the field trip that would last forever.

Chapter Ten

On Saturday morning the girls found Newt examining an anthill at the edge of the backyard. He watched the ants carefully through a magnifying glass, stopping only to make notes in his spiral notebook.

"Want to see a queen up close?" he asked as the girls settled down on the grass beside him.

"Sure," Grey said, taking the magnifying glass for a turn.

"Want to go with us on an adventure?" Sparky asked, anxious to forget the ants and get on with the business at hand.

"What kind of adventure?" he asked without looking up.

Sparky and Grey had already discussed how to get Newt's help without mentioning the magic part. "Well," she explained, choosing her words carefully, "you know we went on a field trip to Grouseland yesterday."

"Been there, done that," Newt said, as he continued to stare at the anthill and jot down his observations. It annoyed Sparky that Newt sometimes paid very little attention to them and their ideas. She sent a look to Grey and bit her lip.

Grey handed the magnifying glass back to the young scientist. "Thank you, Newt. The ants are quite interesting, but Sparky and I have a school project that we'd like you to help us with."

"What kind of school project?"

"It involves a lot of research, and we know how good you are at that," Grey said, knowing how boys like it when people brag on their abilities.

"Tell me more," he said simply.

Grey explained how interested she and Sparky had become in the slaves who worked at Grouseland in its early days, and how a research project would bring them some extra credit in history class. Although she already had an A average in history, she told him, Sparky only had a C+ and the extra credit would probably give her a B. Sparky wasn't sure that she liked this approach, but didn't argue because it was true.

"So we're thinking, if we could do some research on the slaves who worked for the Harrison family, it would be interesting and also be academic."

"So what do you need me for?" Newt asked.

"Because we don't know where to start," Sparky said. "And you always know how to get information."

Newt smiled. "Well, I guess I could put my anthill project on hold for today and give you girls a hand." He stood up and dropped the magnifying glass into the pocket of his cargo pants.

"Great," the girls said in unison.

"Let's start with the library," Newt said. "Bring quarters for the copy machine, just in case."

Within minutes, the three were on their way to the library. They parked their bikes near the wide front steps. Grey carried a pen and notebook and Sparky carried the quarters. Newt wore his backpack in case they needed to haul books home.

Mrs. Brighton, a very short librarian, helped them and soon the three had local history books spread over a table. It was hard not to be distracted by all the information. One book contained early photographs of all the schools and churches in the town. The kids decided that school would have been fun back in the old days, especially when they read about the short school year, so kids could be home to help with farm chores.

"Interesting," Grey said, when she read that school didn't start until after the harvest season and ended when spring planting began. "Such a short school year—it's amazing that anyone learned anything."

"It was probably just like the school in *The Little House on the Prairie,*" Sparky said, "with all the grades in one room sharing one teacher. They used a dipper and a water bucket and had to go outside to use the bathroom. *Brrr*...I bet that got cold in the winter."

"School sure was different back then," Grey said calmly. "That's for sure."

"I would have hated it," Newt said. "No computers."

Sparky shuddered when she read aloud the part about

the hickory switches used by teachers to keep order in the classroom. She knew one of them would have been aimed directly at her.

"Focus, please," Grey said, as she opened a book on the early businesses in the town. She thumbed through pages until she found a reference to Tanner's General Store. She looked eagerly at Sparky, and they remembered Calico's words. The news of the store's existence thrilled the girls, a reminder that they had not just dreamed up the whole thing. However, the small amount of information dampened their enthusiasm somewhat.

Mrs. Brighton wandered by to check on them. "How are you doing?" She smiled, always happy to see children using a Saturday morning for a school project.

"It's all very interesting," Grey said, "but it's just too general." She pointed to the information about the stores. "How could we find out more about a specific store?"

The librarian straightened her glasses and twitched her mouth sideways as she thought. "Well, you might try the Historical Society. They have some items actually used in some of the early businesses, donated by family members. I recall seeing a tin ice cream scoop that dates back to the turn of the century, used in a local ice cream parlor." She paused, then added, "I believe they have an ancient cash register that is even older than that."

"I know where the place is," Newt said. "Over on Elm Street, right?"

"Yes, on the corner by the bookstore, just a few blocks away."

After thanking the librarian and returning the books to the shelves, the children pedaled down the tree-lined streets to the corner building that housed the county historical society.

"Why are you so interested in one specific store?" Newt asked as they parked their bikes near the door. "I thought this was about slaves." He seemed perplexed that the girls had shifted gears without consulting him.

Sparky answered quickly, "We heard a story at Grouseland about a slave who got hanged, because he stole some horses from a man who ran a store." She glanced at Grey and hoped she hadn't said too much, but it was all true and she hadn't mentioned magic or ghosts.

Grey said, "The slave's name was Isaac Washington, and a Russell Tanner owned the store. We thought it would be interesting to find out more about the story."

"*Hmmm*," Newt responded. "I don't recall hearing anything about a hanging last year when my class took the tour."

"Well, we probably had a different guide than you did," Grey said quickly. "You know they're all volunteers, probably a different one every day."

"Yeah," Sparky added. "I bet telling about a hanging would really creep some ladies out, so they'd probably just skip it."

Although Newt shrugged his shoulders and seemed to

accept the explanation, he pulled his eyebrows into a frown at the thought of missing something that important. He promised himself if he ever led a tour, he'd include every tiny detail.

When they opened the front door of the Historical Society, a bell tinkled, announcing their visit. A kind-looking, silver-haired man, sitting at the front desk, smiled at the three young visitors. They smiled back and strolled through the quiet rooms taking in everything. Large murals of early town scenes and portraits in fancy frames lined the walls. One room contained glass cases displaying items from the past. Another room was filled with books and maps. Grey thought it seemed very much like a museum, only smaller. Sparky thought it smelled dusty. Newt thought it didn't have enough science in it.

"May I help you?" asked the silver-haired volunteer, when the kids returned to the front desk.

Grey stepped up to his desk. "Yes, please sir. We are interested in finding out about a general store that was here many years ago, owned by a man named Mr. Russell Tanner."

The old man rubbed his chin as he thought. "Yes, the old Tanner General Store. I don't think we have any pictures of that particular store, but I do have an old city map that shows you right where it stood."

"Do you have any artifacts from the store?" Newt asked, impressing the girls with his use of the word 'artifacts'. He liked reminding them of his age and wisdom.

"I don't think so, but we'll have a look," the man said.

He led them to a case filled with glass bottles, measuring devices, and some old tools. "These aren't from the same store, but they would have been the kind of merchandise Mr. Tanner sold."

"What about his store account book? Would you possibly have that?" Grey asked hopefully.

"Not sure," he mumbled, "but there are some old ledgers in a file in the next room. Let's go look." As he led the way, he added, "Families save these old books, then they bring them to us because they don't know what else to do with them." The girls smiled at each other at the hope of finding the account book mentioned by Calico.

After moving several boxes and checking three file drawers, the man said, "*Aha*! We may be on to something here."

"Did you find it?" asked Grey. She tried to keep the excitement from her voice.

"Well, I found another box of old account books," he said as he dragged the box out into the open space. "Maybe it's in here."

The kids crowded in for a closer look. After dusting and removing the lid, he lifted the old books out and onto a nearby table. He examined each one and then laid it to the side. Finally, when he picked up the last book, he said, "I believe I may have found it."

"Hurray," chorused the girls.

"Yes, I think this is exactly what you're looking for," he said with a grin. Then he carefully placed the account book from Mr. Russell Tanner's store in front of the children.

"Be very careful; it's fragile," he warned.

Newt moved away to examine some ancient medical tools, while the girls carefully turned the pages of the old book. Faded, swirling script listed dates and sales. Some of the pages had come loose, and the girls turned them gently so they wouldn't fall out of place. They wondered how long it had been since anyone had looked at this book that kept track of daily sales and expenses in Tanner's General Store.

The earliest entry was on January 1, 1809. They wondered if that marked the day Russell Tanner opened the store, or just the day he started this particular account book. It didn't matter, so they kept turning pages until they came to the date that Calico had told them: June 3, 1810–her birthday.

It started like every other page with the date, and although it seemed strange to the girls, Mr. Tanner had kept a record of the weather on each page. Grey said that made it more like a journal as he recorded his life in the store. That particular day had been warm and sunny.

When Grey moved her fingers down the sales listed on June 3, 1810, the girls saw he had sold a bucket, a pair of suspenders, a gallon of molasses, a box of nails, 20 pounds of chicken feed, and a bolt of flannel cloth. Their eyes widened when they came to the next item: a doll, 25 cents. They knew it had to be the doll that Calico's father bought her for her birthday. Quickly, they left the column of items sold and ran their fingers down to the bottom of the page, to the list of daily expenses. Sure enough, he'd written that 25 cents had been paid to a man named Isaac for moving some horses.

"Yes," said Grey.

"We found it, Newt," Sparky called.

The girls jumped away from the table and high-fived each other in joy. Then they dragged Newt over to have a look at their discovery.

Newt couldn't quite understand the girls' excitement over finding the information, but then he wasn't always on the same page with them anymore, since he was older, so it didn't matter. His mind had probably already wandered back to his anthill project.

"Let's make a copy," Grey said.

The kindly volunteer made a copy of the page for the girls' school project, gave them an extra copy, slipped both copies into a folder, and didn't even charge them for it. Grey thanked him for his generosity, while Sparky dropped a quarter into the donation can on his desk.

"Now what?" Newt asked as they straightened up their bikes to go.

Grey asked, "Where could we find information about a hanging?" Sparky shivered at the thought and admired Grey for her cool detachment.

"Let's see...that would have to be recorded with the court records—at the courthouse," Newt said with authority. "It's never open on Saturday, though."

"Let's go right after school on Monday, okay?" Grey asked.

"Good for me," Newt said.

"Me too," said Sparky.

The date settled, they realized they were halfway there. The girls glanced at each other and giggled with excitement.

As soon as the girls got home from school on Monday afternoon, they whistled for Newt.

"I'm coming, I'm coming," he yelled from the top of the stairs leading to his apartment. "Boy, you girls don't give a guy much time for a snack after school."

"Bring it with you," Sparky called.

"All done," he said as he skipped down the steps and dropped a banana peel into the trashcan at the bottom of the stairs. He wiped his hands on his T-shirt. "Let's go."

The girls followed as Newt led the way to the big county courthouse, sitting like a castle on a knoll in the middle of the town. They parked their bikes in the bike racks near the back door.

Newt and the girls marched up the steps and into the cool block building. They passed the office of the county treasurer. "I come here with my father occasionally to pay taxes and stuff," he said with authority.

The three children walked slowly down the wide hallway reading the signs over the doors. Several people doing business passed them briskly, but paid no attention to them.

"In some ways, it's a lot easier to investigate matters when you're a kid," Newt told them as they walked. "Adults usually ignore kids, thinking they are just goofing around. That gives kids the advantage to snoop about and even eavesdrop without being noticed."

Sparky smiled. She liked the idea of snooping around and eavesdropping.

"Here it is," Grey said when she spotted the sign over the next door: Court Records. They approached the counter and apparently disturbed a plump, blonde secretary at her computer.

"*A-hem!*" Newt cleared his throat rather loudly to get her attention.

She looked at the children crossly and said, "We don't make donations here." She immediately turned back to her computer.

"Excuse us," Grey said politely, "but we aren't asking for donations. We would like to see the court records for June, 1810."

The woman looked surprised at the request from three kids. She took a drink from a can of soda on her desk, then pulled her reading glasses to the end of her nose and peered over them at the children. Slowly, she pushed her chair back from her computer, got up, and walked to the counter where the three children patiently waited.

"You want to see court records?" she asked, sounding somewhat surprised at the request.

"Yes, please," Grey said. "For June, 1810."

Sparky spoke up. "It's for a school project."

Newt added, "It's public information. We have a right to see it."

Leave it to Newt to know something like that, the girls thought. They hoped the woman didn't think he was being rude. They watched her eyes, but her expression didn't change.

"All right, you can see it, but it has to stay right here in the office," she said in a grumpy voice. "Come on around here." She motioned for them to enter her area and then pointed to a wooden table with four chairs around it.

"What was the date again?" she asked.

"June, 1810," Newt said. Suddenly he seemed more interested.

Amazingly, it didn't take very long. The woman left and returned with a book, opened to June. She laid it on the table before them and returned to her computer. The kids scooted their chairs forward and began to examine the book of court activities.

"Find June 3rd," Sparky said as Grey's fingers moved through the pages.

"Here it is," Grey said, laying the pages open to expose the court activities that took place on June 3, 1810.

"*Hmmm*," she said, after scanning the page. "Nothing about Calico's father."

She moved on to June 4th. The other two watched her fingers as she traced down the lines until she found: State versus Isaac Washington.

"Here it is."

"All right," Sparky said excitedly.

They silently read through the paragraph of testimony accusing Isaac Washington of horse stealing, which they decided must have been a very serious crime back then. Two witnesses were listed: Mr. Jake Phillips and Mr. George McCulley. Further down the page they found the names of twelve jury members, all men. Under that, in a line all by itself: Verdict: Guilty. They gasped when they read the sentence: To be hanged by the neck until dead. A shiver passed through them as they exchanged glances.

"Here, read this part," Newt said. He pointed to a section lower on the page.

Grey moved her fingers down and they all read the next part: Site of execution: Shady Rest Cemetery. "The cemetery on the edge of town."

Their teachers had told them about graves there dating back to the 1790's.

"Don't you get it?" Newt said. "The hanged him in the cemetery right over his grave. Zip–drop–right into the hole." The girls were shocked just thinking about it. They gulped and moved on down to read the last entry regarding the execution: Costs to County: $18.10. Listed beneath those words was an itemized list detailing the expense of a rope, a shirt, a shroud, a scaffold, and wages paid to the gravedigger.

"So you see, Newt," Sparky said, "if the store owner paid him to move the horses, then he didn't steal them."

Grey held up her folder of pages from the historical society. "Look at this. We have proof right here that Mr. Tanner gave him a quarter to move the horses."

Newt considered the facts. "I wonder why Mr. Tanner didn't testify in his behalf."

"Maybe he was dead," Sparky said quickly.

"Or maybe he left town right after he gave Isaac the quarter. Then they couldn't have talked to him, and he would have missed the trial," Grey said thoughtfully.

"You know they didn't have cell phones back then," Sparky added.

"Notice this part," Grey said, pointing to the court record. "His trial was on June 4th and they hanged him on June 5th."

"Wow! Not much time to line up any defense," Newt said with a scowl.

"Wouldn't it be great if we could clear his name?" Grey said. She glanced at Sparky.

"Yeah, that would be an A+ school project, for sure," Sparky said.

"Cool," Newt said with a grin. "We can do it! Let's make some copies of this information. This is more than a school project. This is a noble cause." Newt was on board now and the girls loved it.

"What should we do next?" they asked.

Newt squinted through his glasses at the girls. "My dad has a friend who is an investigative reporter. Let's get him to help us. He loves this kind of stuff."

Not only did the newsman love the story, but he wrote a half page article about it in the local newspaper, complete with pictures of the three children. The article hailed them as heroes for a brief time in their town and at school. Although they were always a bit fuzzy about where they came up with the idea for the whole thing, people didn't care. It became a grand project with justice served, and that made the grown-ups feel good.

The *Indianapolis Star* picked up the story and it reached a much wider audience than anyone expected. One day a call came from a relative of Isaac Washington. Mr. Orville H. Washington, a far-distant grandson and attorney in Atlanta, Georgia, read the article. He called the Bailey home and asked to speak to the girls.

Mom, who had answered the phone, called the girls down from their room. Sparky, being too nervous to talk, pushed Grey toward the phone.

"Hello, my name is Greyling Bailey," Grey said somewhat nervously.

"And I'm Sparky," Sparky called into the phone they attempted to share.

"Hello, girls," the deep voice came through loud and

clear. "My name is Orville Washington, and I am Isaac Washington's grandson with many greats in front of it."

The girls giggled as they shared the phone, heads pressed together.

He continued, "On behalf of the whole Washington family, I want to thank you for finding this valuable information for us. I'm not sure how you stumbled onto it, but we are extremely grateful."

"You are welcome," Grey said. "We are happy about it too."

"It was a school project," Sparky yelled into the phone.

Grey nudged her to be quiet.

"I intend to take this information to the Governor, and seek a pardon for Isaac. I think he will hear me and will officially clear his name."

The girls jumped up and down with glee, almost dropping the phone.

"I will send that information to your local paper as soon as it takes place," Mr. Orville Washington promised.

"Good-bye, sir," Grey said politely.

"And thank you very much," Sparky called into the phone.

Surprisingly, it didn't take very long. A few weeks later, the good news came in a letter addressed to the girls and Newt. It thanked them for their patriotic duty and was signed by the Governor of the state. A reporter from the local newspaper came and took a of picture of the three children holding the letter. The picture and story appeared on the front page of the Sunday edition. Of course, with the extra credit they all ended up getting A's in history. Although Grey received an A+ and Newt got an A, Sparky was delighted with her A-. Their families were very proud of them.

Mom called it an act of kindness, and Dad said they'd probably grow up and work for the F.B.I. someday. Miss Dooley called them good citizens and told the other children they should follow their examples.

The last step of the journey was to take the information to Calico, the little ghost girl at Grouseland. Sparky and Grey couldn't invite Newt to accompany them, so they biked without him to the historic mansion on a cloudy Saturday morning in May.

They fell into line behind a group of visitors waiting for a tour. Calico waited for them at the exact same spot where they had first seen her. Exchanging smiles, they waited until everyone else left the area. No longer afraid, they approached the little spirit. When they had shared the newspaper pictures and the letter, tears came into her eyes.

"It makes me so happy. I don't know how to thank you."

"You don't need to. We are pleased we could help you," Grey said.

"Now you can go on to Heaven," Sparky said.

"Yes, now I can proudly go and be with my family."

"You can take these with you, to show them," Sparky said, handing her the folder containing copies of the letter and newspaper articles.

Calico smiled widely and hugged the folder to her chest.

Sparky wondered just how many things you could take to Heaven with you, and if you could take things, then why didn't people put more in the coffins of loved ones. Grey wondered if Calico and her parents could read, and if people who couldn't read in life would suddenly be able to read in death. But those questions had no answers.

Calico wiggled her fingers in a good-bye wave at the girls, and then she was gone.

That night the girls sat on their beds and discussed the whole event and the many other overwhelming things that had occurred since they had been together. They remembered the vow they had made to Rupa, the Gypsy woman, to be brave and to always use their gift to help others. Although they still didn't understand why they had this special gift, they accepted it as real and true, something to be treasured forever. Touching hands, they shared a warm feeling that they *had* done something good, something that had helped others. As Grey and Sparky held hands, they made a solemn promise to always be fair and honest, to always look for good causes, and to always keep the secret of Bailey's Chase.

Marlis Day loved reading books about adventurous kids when she was a child. Like Sparky and Grey Bailey, she enjoyed riding her bike around looking for a mystery to solve. She imagined having dangerous and magical adventures like the two girl heroines in the town of Bailey's Chase.

When she was an adult, she became a teacher and read exciting books to all of her students. She wrote three mysteries for adults. This is her first book for middle-age kids. She hopes they will delight in it.

The author lives with her husband in the rolling hills of southern Indiana where she is working on the next book about Sparky and Grey Bailey. She loves to visit schools and read to kids.

Made in the USA
Lexington, KY
14 July 2017